9/26/08

By Michael de Guzman

Melonhead
Beekman's Big Deal
The Bamboozlers
Finding Stinko

FINDING STINKO

Michael de Guzman

FINDING STINKO

FARRAR, STRAUS and GIROUX

NEW YORK

Library of Congress Cataloging-in-Publication Data
De Guzman, Michael.
    Finding Stinko / Michael de Guzman.— 1st ed.
       p.   cm.
    Summary: Having spent his life trying to escape the foster care system,
eventually becoming mute to keep out of trouble, twelve-year-old Newboy
finally hits the streets, where a discarded ventriloquist's dummy gives him
back his voice and his hope.
    ISBN-13: 978-0-374-32305-9
    ISBN-10: 0-374-32305-4
    [1. Mutism, elective—Fiction.   2. Ventriloquism—Fiction.   3. Dolls—Fiction.
4. Runaways—Fiction.   5. Foster home care—Fiction.]   I. Title.

PZ7.D3655 Fin 2007
[Fic]—dc22

2006040859

To my daughters

With thanks to W.A.

FINDING STINKO

Prologue / Newboy

The girl, who was no more than fifteen and maybe younger, stood beneath an overhang watching the back entrance to the apartment building. Rain pellets the size of dimes smacked the concrete of the alley, which was cracked and land-mined with potholes. It was a world of potholes, the girl thought. A large doorman in a heavy raincoat and hat stood guard. Two such men guarded the front of the building. Their job was to keep out whoever didn't belong. The girl had dark hair and dark eyes. She was tall and thin. Her street name was Roo, because she was flighty and bounced when she ran. She cradled something beneath her coat, which retarded neither wet nor cold.

Roo had been casing the building since yesterday, sizing up its residents as they came and went, trying to find the way in. Rich people lived inside. This was her best chance. Maybe her only chance. Yesterday a car had come and the rear doorman had gone off. It had only been for a few minutes. That was all she needed.

The bundle stirred and she pulled it tighter to her chest, which was hardly more than thin-skinned bone. The small car splashed past her and stopped. The doorman got in and it drove off. Roo darted across the alley and down the stairs to the basement. The door was unlocked. She hurried along a corridor, then up a flight of stairs. She pulled at the heavy metal door until it opened an inch. She peeked in and saw a large room filled with palm trees in pots and plush chairs and couches. On the far side she saw a man in a maroon uniform with gold braid standing by a set of glass doors. His attention was directed to the street.

She slipped into the lobby and set her bundle on the seat cushion of a large chair that was mostly hidden behind a palm. Her son was sleeping. His tiny face was covered still with the fuzz of birth. He was wrapped in a dirty blanket. She set the note she'd written next to him.

THIS IS MY SON, she'd printed in fastidious, childlike block letters. HIS NAME IS NEWBOY. HE IS ONE WEEK OLD. PLEASE TAKE CARE OF HIM. I CAN'T.

Roo kissed her son. "I love you," she whispered. She kissed him again. Then once more. She retreated to watch from behind the metal door. She hoped to see who would save him. She fought the urge to take him back, to find some way to do it herself. She hadn't wanted to live on the streets. Or have a child. She couldn't nurse. She had no way to feed him. No way to offer comfort.

An elevator door opened and a middle-aged couple emerged. Roo held her breath. The man in maroon and gold opened the glass doors for them, and the couple disappeared. She could wait no more. She hurried down the stairs and up into the alley, her eyes pooled with tears. She'd named her son Newboy because he was starting out new. All she wanted was for his life to be better than her own.

Newboy was reasonably well tended to as an infant in the state child-care system. That he received only fleeting personal attention was the result of always being one of too many. He was small and slow to develop. He didn't start crawling until he was eighteen months old. He observed everything and reacted to nothing. He didn't cry. Not even when he fell down the stairs and cut his chin, which left a scar. His permanent expression seemed never-endingly sad. Nobody adopted him.

When he turned two, his left eye began to wander, as though it was searching for something the other one couldn't see. He spent hours staring out the window, as though expecting somebody to appear. Mrs. Higgis, who ran the foster home he was living in then, secured his ankle to a radiator with six feet of clothesline after he tried to escape. He worked himself free and tried again. He was caught crawling down the middle of the street. Mrs. Higgis sent him back to the state orphanage.

The adults in whose care Newboy was placed weren't

all bad, or even indifferent to their responsibilities. The Eustices, for example, treated him like family. He took his first steps at their urging. He spoke his first word, "More." He was pointing at the mashed potatoes. All of his first words were related to food. Mrs. Eustice read him stories. He grew. He started tripping over his feet, which were pigeon-toed and much too long for the rest of him. The Eustices got divorced and Newboy was returned.

He spent six months at a large state facility, then another six with people named Kastle, who yelled at one another all day long.

If there was a theme to Newboy's existence, it was his commitment to escape. He made the attempt everywhere he lived. This passion for freedom was entered into his record when he was four. From then on he was watched more carefully. When he was five, the Bicks took him. They fed their boys two meals a day, heavy on the starch. Newboy complained about being hungry. The next day he was fed one meal. He complained again. The next day he was fed nothing. From then on he said only what he had to. He watched and listened. He blended into the routine until he was hardly noticed. Until he could be in a room alone without somebody asking him what he was up to.

When the opportunity came, he was ready. Mrs. Bick was out. Mr. Bick was upstairs unclogging a toilet. The other boys were doing yard work. He climbed on a chair, tugged open the window, turned so he could go out feet-first, lost his grip, and fell into a rosebush. Mr. Bick extracted the thorns with needle-nose pliers. Newboy was replaced with a less troublesome boy.

The houses Newboy lived in were scattered about at the edges of the city where he'd been born. Once these neighborhoods had been working middle class. Now they were run-down. He moved from one situation to another with a few changes of clothes, an extra pair of sneakers if he was lucky, socks, underwear, and a coat. He outgrew things too quickly to accumulate much. He possessed nothing personal, not a photograph, not a single remembrance. He didn't trust adults. His existence was about survival and being free.

He lived with the Hinklesons for a while, one of two foster boys in a house that was always neat and clean. Everything in its place. Including the inhabitants. He was enrolled in second grade. His teacher, Mr. Gleason, took him on as a project. Newboy started reading and liking it. The Hinklesons moved to another state and Newboy was sent to another foster home. In his next school, he was labeled difficult, stubborn, a lost cause.

When he was eight, Newboy's mother crept into his thoughts. He tried to imagine what she looked like. He decided that she had dark hair like his, and his deep brown eyes. He was certain that she'd lost him, and that it wasn't her fault. He knew she was out there looking for him.

He grew six inches that year. His feet remained too long for the rest of him. He kept tripping over them. He

stole a bicycle in a desperate attempt to get away. He discovered the brakes didn't work while he was speeding
down a hill. He crashed into a curb and was thrown
headlong into a ditch, breaking his nose, his right wrist,
three ribs, and his left clavicle. He vowed never again to
take things that didn't belong to him.

When he was nine, Newboy stopped talking. He didn't
do it on purpose. It wasn't something he desired. He just
opened his mouth one morning and nothing came out.
Not a word. No matter how hard he tried. The Snipeses,
who'd had him only a week when it happened, were per-
plexed, then angry. His teachers became frustrated. So
did Newboy. He gave up trying.

"So what if I can't speak out loud?" Newboy said inside his head. "What do I care? I'll talk to myself instead."

He started writing what he had to say on a pad of paper he carried with him. The school didn't like it. The
Snipeses didn't like it. Newboy was sent back to the state.
The state sent him to a doctor, who examined him from
end to end.

"There's nothing physically wrong with you," the doctor said.

He was sent to a psychologist, who analyzed him, then
reanalyzed him. Newboy wrote the answers to her questions, but nothing that explained his silence. How could
he explain what he didn't understand? In any event, he
revealed as little as possible. He studied inkblots and
wrote down that they looked like inkblots. He fitted

round objects into round openings and square ones into square.

"A chicken could do this," Newboy said inside his head.

He was attached to a machine that read brain waves.

"You may or may not talk again," the psychologist said when she was done.

He was visited by a pleasant man from the state department of education, who tested him, then retested him. His IQ was average. He read at the fourth-grade level, which was the grade he was in. Another family, the Livermores, agreed to give him a try.

One night, not long afterward, something happened that gave Newboy hope. He saw Harpo Marx in a movie on television. Harpo's brothers were in it too, but it was the man with the long curls and top hat who didn't talk that caught his attention. When Harpo wanted to say something, he honked his horn. When he honked his horn, people paid attention.

"Someday," Newboy said inside his head, "I'm going to honk a horn of my own."

It would take a while, and there would be many failed attempts at escape before it happened. But it did.

Three years later . . .

1 / Hard Knox

The military nature of the foster establishment run by Mr. and Mrs. Knox was a big problem for Newboy. Mrs. Knox wrote a daily schedule. Mr. Knox posted it on the corkboard by the doorless doorways to the two rooms where the boys slept, three to a room. The schedule told them where to be and when to be there and what they were supposed to do.

Wake-up was at 5:30, 6:30 on weekends. Breakfast was a half hour later. That lasted twenty minutes. Cleanup lasted ten. They had half an hour to make their beds and clean their rooms. There was another half hour of general chores. At 7:30 on weekdays, Mr. Knox drove them to school in the green van. At 3:30 he picked them up. They were monitored closely by teachers in between. At 4:00 the boys resumed their household chores. Dinner was at 6:00. Cleanup and homework followed. Bedtime was at 9:30. Weekend nights they were allowed an hour of television if they'd all been good.

Newboy's big problem was alone time. There wasn't any. The boys were supervised by one of the Knoxes, or they supervised each other by working in pairs. If one of them broke a rule or misbehaved or didn't do the job the way it was supposed to be done, both boys were punished. Punishment was swift and severe. Mrs. Knox decided what it would be. Mr. Knox administered the prescribed dosage. The other boys lived in constant fear. If one of them saw Newboy attempting to escape, he'd sound the alarm in an instant.

Newboy had spent weeks figuring the best way out. He'd run each possible scenario through his mind's eye, watching himself test each exit and fail, abandoning each until in the end he came to a single conclusion. He'd have one chance. He'd woken up knowing that this was the day he'd take it.

Sitting in the backseat of the green van after school, Newboy reviewed his plan. He took himself through it step by step. He pictured every obstacle and the action he'd have to take to get past it.

"How was school today, boys?" Mr. Knox asked. He asked them every day. He was a deliberate man with a fixed mind, a slow mover, a reptile on a cold day.

"Good," one of them said. It was as much of an answer as they'd give. In the system, a boy learned not to volunteer information. Never use two words when one would do.

Newboy couldn't have answered if he'd wanted to,

which he didn't. His voice was still missing. "I did nothing in school today," he said inside his head. "Like always." They'd put him in a class for the kids with special needs.

"School's important, boys," Mr. Knox said.

"Here it comes," Newboy said inside his head.

"You don't stand a chance without a good education," Mr. Knox said.

"Which you'll never get," Newboy said inside his head, mimicking Mr. Knox's high-pitched whine to perfection.

"Which you'll never get," Mr. Knox said. He snickered.

The Knoxes made a business of their boys. For each foster kid in their care, they received a monthly check from the state to reimburse them for room, board, clothes, and living expenses. It was no secret to the boys that much of that money was added to what Mr. Knox made from his part-time job, and that the Knoxes worked tirelessly to hide the fact and to present the authorities with a rosy picture. On their occasional visits, state inspectors were treated like royalty, with both the boys and the house scrubbed and polished. Which was why the Knoxes were permitted to look after such a large number of wards.

Mrs. Knox handled the paperwork. Tonight it was a form with Newboy's name on it. Before dinner she sat Newboy down at the oversize kitchen table, which looked like it belonged in a school cafeteria.

"The state wants a progress report," she said, making it sound like it was his fault. "Well, we know how to take care of the state, don't we?" She was roly-poly, with a kindly face.

"Tell them I'm gone," Newboy said inside his head. "Tell them to forget me."

"You're still not talking, I take it?" she said. She always made it sound like he was faking.

"I wouldn't talk to you if I could," Newboy said inside his head.

"I've got you until you're eighteen," Mrs. Knox said. "That's six more years. You'll be talking before that. You'll be doing lots of things you're not doing now." She filled in a section of the form.

She'd tell the state that he was making progress. He knew that. He knew she'd tell them he was happy. She'd make it up, then read it to him so he could feel worse about the truth of his circumstances. She took obvious pleasure in this.

Dinner was macaroni and cheese. Newboy did his homework and showed it to Mr. Knox, as each boy had to do. Newboy suspected that Mr. Knox couldn't read very well because it took him such a long time to get through a page, no matter what was on it. Mr. Knox always said the homework wasn't up to snuff, no matter how good it was.

After that, Newboy read his much-used copy of *Robin-*

son Crusoe until lights-out. He'd brought it with him from the last place. It was a pocket-sized hardcover edition, printed in London in 1923. Newboy often marveled that such an old thing could have survived all these years and made its way to him.

2 / At Last!

It was just after midnight. Newboy stood at the top of the stairs looking down, clenching a plastic shopping bag filled with all his possessions. The other boys were sleeping. The house was quiet. He held his breath and started working his five-foot-seven-inch string bean of a body cautiously onto the first step.

"I'm going to trip over my feet," he said inside his head. His feet were size eleven. "I'm going to fall and break a leg and wake everybody up." He allowed the weight of one foot to settle before bringing the other to join it.

He made his way down three steps without creating the whisper of a sound; then his right toe caught on his left heel and he started tipping forward, slowly, the way a tree leans just before the fall. His right leg reached out into the nothingness of space. He spun himself around like a corkscrew. His left foot found solid wood. His right foot came down by its side. His free hand found the wall. He held his balance. He held his breath. He listened.

Mrs. Knox was still snoring.

He made his way down another step. Then another. His movement on the stairs sounded to him like pig squeals and thunderclaps. Newboy was acutely aware of sound. He could hear things that were far away. Sometimes he could hear a cat walking on grass.

The Knoxes' bedroom was just below. They slept with their door open. One creak too many and Mrs. Knox would be out of bed faster than an agitated rattlesnake. He took the last step. He stood as still as he knew how outside their room. He heard snorts of air escaping Mrs. Knox's mouth, like tiny puffs of smoke. Beneath him, under the flooring, a wooden beam groaned.

"She's going to hear me," Newboy said inside his head. "She's going to tell him to beat me." He stepped over the floorboards he knew would protest his presence the loudest. He made his way through the kitchen in the dark, navigating from memory. He pulled the bolt, unfastened the chain, and released the lock. He pushed the door open firmly and quickly so that its hinges wouldn't squawk. Mrs. Knox kept them unoiled on purpose. The slower they were opened, the more noise they made.

He moved quickly along the side of the old clapboard house. He ducked beneath the Knoxes' bedroom window. He threw his plastic bag over the eight-foot fence that separated the backyard from the front. His fingers found the top of the fence and interlaced themselves with its twisted metal ends. The sharp points pricked at his hands as he climbed. His jacket caught on one of the twists. He tugged at it. It wouldn't come free.

"I'm going to pull too hard and rip it," he said inside his head. He tugged at it again, then pulled harder. He had to get going. He yanked as hard as he could and the jacket came free, ripping along one side from the pocket to the collar, exposing the lining. He jumped to the ground, fell, grabbed his bag, and started running. If he was lucky, they wouldn't start looking for him until wake-up. But they *would* come looking. The state didn't like to hear that a boy in foster care was missing. The Knoxes weren't about to lose their lucrative business.

Newboy took his bearings and headed for the city. He could see the tops of its tallest buildings sticking up like lighthouses some ten miles distant. His heart pounded with excitement. And fear. If Mrs. Knox had been roused from her sleep by an attack of intestinal combustion—a common occurrence—she could be upstairs checking on the boys right now. She could already be looking for him.

From time to time he lost sight of the tall buildings and his spirits sank. Without the buildings he didn't know where he was going. When they appeared again as he came over a hill, he rejoiced. Each time he found them again, he was closer.

He walked quickly, the plastic bag swinging at his side. A single change of clothes, a bar of soap, a small towel, his toothbrush, a half-filled tube of toothpaste, his book, the pad and ballpoint pen he used to write notes were all that weighed it down. He had twenty-seven dollars and forty cents, the amount he'd managed to gather and hide over the past several years. The Knoxes ran the eleventh foster home Newboy had lived in since his birth. He was determined that it would be his last.

3 / He Speaks

A maze of neighborhoods separated Newboy from his immediate destination. Streets stopped at dead ends, and he was never sure which way to go. Sometimes he had to double back before he could move on. He hurried, but he didn't run. He tried to remember what he knew of the city from his infrequent trips there: school outings to museums and factories, recovery time in the hospital, a night at a ball game once. Now he had to find a place to hide while he decided what to do.

The half-moon was setting over the hill to his west as he crossed the drawbridge that connected neighborhoods north of the river to the city's urban core. He made his way up the hill to his east, which overlooked the mass of skyscrapers and the river that ran through them. At the top of the hill he reached Broadway, a street that was lined for nearly a mile with a seemingly endless array of businesses. A twenty-four-hour copy center and an all-night diner were both crowded. A police car appeared from a side street.

Newboy knew he'd made a mistake the moment he started running. The Knoxes wouldn't tell the cops he was missing. They'd come after him themselves. He was property they owned. If he'd just kept walking, the cops probably would have ignored him. Now he had to worry about being caught and identified.

In five long strides, Newboy's pigeon-toed feet straightened themselves out and he was galloping like the favorite to win the Kentucky Derby. He tore up a narrow street, past a church, through its cemetery to another yard, across another street, and into an alley. He listened. No car was on the prowl. He was safe. For the moment. He needed a place to spend the rest of the night. Someplace warm if possible. Someplace dry. It was beginning to snow.

The Dumpster sat behind an apartment building in the glow of a security light. It was filled with garbage. Newboy climbed in. He tried to find comfort. Something was wedged in his back. He pulled it free and found himself staring at the dim outline of a face. He could feel that its left ear had been chewed off, and that its right eye was permanently closed, and that the tip of its nose was missing. The face was attached to a body that had arms but no hands. The doll was about two feet tall and wore the remnants of a jacket, shirt, long pants, and plastic shoes.

Newboy started to throw it to the other side of the

Dumpster, then decided to examine it more closely. He discovered that if he pushed down on its lower lip, its mouth moved. When he let the lip go, its mouth snapped shut. He turned the doll over. The jacket and shirt were open in the back. Its body was hollow above the waist. He put his hand inside and felt a string with a loop at the end of it. The other end disappeared into the doll's head.

He put a finger into the loop and pulled on it.

The doll's mouth opened. "I'm Newboy," the doll said in Newboy's voice.

Newboy wasn't aware that he'd spoken. The sound of his voice after all this time startled him. When he realized that he'd talked, he was stunned. As suddenly as he'd stopped, he'd begun again. He withdrew his finger from the loop. He opened his mouth to say something. Nothing came out. He tried again. He couldn't say a word.

He put his finger back into the loop and pulled. "I'm Newboy," the doll said in Newboy's voice.

"Why can I talk with the doll, but not by myself?" Newboy asked inside his head. He tried again to speak without the doll. He tried singing. He tried yelling. Without moving the doll's mouth, he couldn't make a sound.

He pulled on the loop. "If I can't talk by myself," Newboy had the doll say, "I can have you talk for me." He brought the doll's face closer to his own. "People will look at you when I speak. They won't remember me."

The doll's open eye stared at him dully. It was lifeless

when Newboy wasn't pulling on the loop and speaking. They were speechless without each other.

"I'm going to call you Stinko," Newboy said inside his head. "Because of where I found you."

"Stinko's good," Newboy had Stinko say. "I like it." Newboy was delighted with the prospect of being able to talk again, even in this strange way. He and Stinko could have a regular conversation, like people. What difference did it make if he was holding both ends of it? He'd talk inside his head, and Stinko would talk out loud.

"Newboy and Stinko," he had Stinko say. "Stinko and Newboy." It occurred to him that if Stinko was going to do the talking, Newboy would have to keep his own mouth from moving while he was doing it. As much as possible. Otherwise he'd draw attention to himself. He had to practice.

"My name is Stinko," he had Stinko say. "I'll have pancakes, eggs, sausages, and bacon for breakfast. I'd like two scoops of chocolate ice cream, please. What's the best way to get out of here?"

4 / Stinko

Newboy climbed out of the Dumpster into the gray dawn, Stinko in hand. Between trying to talk without moving his mouth and worrying about his situation, he hadn't slept an hour. A thin crust of snow covered everything like vanilla frosting.

In the first light of day, Newboy could see that Stinko's face was dirty and that his feet were on backward. He tried to turn them around, but they wouldn't budge.

"Somebody didn't like you," Newboy said inside his head. "I know about that." He slipped his finger into the loop.

"Good morning, Newboy," he had Stinko say.

"Good morning, Stinko," Newboy said inside his head.

He tried to coordinate the doll's mouth movements with his own. He clenched his teeth in an effort to keep his lips from moving.

"My name is Stinko," he had Stinko say. It came out

sounding like Frankenstein's monster speaking with a mouthful of marbles. He kept practicing. "How do we get out of the city? Where do we go?"

"I don't know where we're going," Newboy said inside his head.

"The Knoxes will find you if we don't get out of here fast," he had Stinko say.

"I'm trying to figure it out," Newboy said inside his head.

"Let's just start going," he had Stinko say.

"We can't just start," Newboy said inside his head. "I have to know where we're going first." He slipped his finger out of the loop, withdrawing his hand from Stinko's back.

He broke the ice at the surface of a pothole in the alley. He cupped water into his hand and washed his face. He brushed his teeth. He ran a wet hand through his hair. He dampened a corner of his towel and washed Stinko's face. It didn't do much good. After repacking his plastic bag, he zipped Stinko inside his jacket and the two new friends stole away.

Two blocks farther on, Newboy caught sight of his reflection in a window. His clothes were filthy. The rip in his jacket was larger. "I'm not going to end up like this," he said inside his head. "I'm not going to live on the streets."

He unzipped his jacket enough to reveal Stinko's battered face. He studied the two of them in the glass, face atop face, like they were part of a totem pole.

"I don't know which one of us looks worse," he said inside his head. He pulled his left arm free of its sleeve and found the loop in Stinko's back.

"If you leave me in your jacket the way I am now," he had Stinko say, "people will look down at me and forget about you."

"Unzip my jacket and there you are," Newboy said inside his head. "Zip it up and you're gone."

"If I'm inside your jacket," Stinko said, "you'll be able to get away faster if you have to run. Let's start walking and see where we end up."

"First we eat," Newboy said inside his head.

"Yeah," Stinko said. "I'm starving."

Newboy thought that was pretty funny. He thought a lot of things were funny. He just never laughed. He started to thread his arm back into its sleeve, then decided to leave it where it was. If he kept his finger in the loop all the time, he could have Stinko ready to talk in an instant.

5 / Broadway

Lights were being turned on. Doors were being unlocked. Sidewalks were being shoveled and salted. Grocery stores, drugstores, banks, bagel shops, smoke shops, bars, restaurants that featured food from Greece and Ethiopia and China and Turkey and Japan and Mexico and Thailand and Italy and Brazil, ice cream parlors, coffee bars, bookstores, beauty salons, and flower stalls were in various stages of getting ready for the day's business. Newboy took it all in as he walked. He saw where he could get a tattoo and a check cashed and a loan. He saw where he could have breakfast.

"What'll you have?" the man behind the counter of the coffee shop asked Newboy. He was skinny, with slicked-back hair and a mustache that looked like it had been painted on.

Newboy unzipped the top of his jacket.

"I'll have the special in the window," Stinko said as his head appeared. "Two fried eggs, fried potatoes, two slices of toast for a dollar twenty-nine." Newboy's mouth moved all over the place while Stinko placed his order.

"You crazy?" the counterman asked Newboy. "We don't serve crazy people."

"I'm just hungry," Stinko said.

Newboy put two dollars on the counter to show that he could pay.

"The special," Stinko said. ".Please."

"Everybody is crazy these days," the counterman said, heading toward the kitchen to place the order. "They all come in here."

"I'm not crazy," Stinko said.

Newboy was sitting at one end of the counter. Three men sat near the other end reading newspapers. Two of the booths that lined the side wall were occupied by couples.

"The state thought I was crazy," Newboy said inside his head. "They thought that was why I stopped talking. I don't know why I stopped talking. I don't know why I can talk using you. But I am not crazy."

"You're not crazy," Stinko said.

"They gave me all those tests," Newboy said inside his head. "I passed them. They couldn't send me to the mental hospital."

"You don't want to go to the mental hospital," Stinko said.

Newboy saw the three men at the end of the counter watching him. The counterman stared at Stinko.

"There's nothing wrong with us," Stinko said.

Newboy zipped his jacket. "I have to get a lot better at this," he said inside his head. He kept his eye on the door while he ate. He knew the Knoxes were out there somewhere in their green van looking for him. In time they'd make it to the city, and to Broadway. They'd ask questions. They'd show his photograph. He figured he had a day, maybe two before they got this far. He yawned in the middle of chewing a mouthful of potatoes. He caught himself nodding off with a slice of toast in his hand. If he didn't get some sleep, he'd pass out.

He dabbed the last stub of toast into the last puddle of egg yolk. He wiped the toast around the plate until all trace of anything edible was gone. He picked up his change, leaving a quarter behind. He used the men's room and left.

He made his way off Broadway. A half dozen streets later, he came upon an abandoned warehouse. Its doors and windows were boarded over with rotting rectangles of plywood. He walked the perimeter to make sure nobody else was around. He pried at a board until it came loose. He lowered himself in through the window to the basement, then pulled the board back into position as tightly as he could. He listened. Nothing stirred. He lay down on the concrete floor. The cold and damp rose to fill his body. In thirty seconds he was sleeping.

6 / Peeper

It was a whomping sort of sound that woke Newboy, like somebody was banging on the floor somewhere high above.

"Let's see what it is," Stinko said when Newboy's finger pulled the loop.

"No way," Newboy said inside his head. "We're getting out of here."

"It's got to be something interesting," Stinko said. "Don't you want to know?"

"It's trouble, is what it is," Newboy said inside his head. He heard the shriek of rubber tires and the crunch of metal meeting metal several blocks away. A fender bender, he thought.

"We'll take a fast look, then go," Stinko said.

"We'll get something to eat, then hit the road," Newboy said inside his head.

"That's what you said the last time we ate," Stinko said. "We're never going to get out of here."

"This time we'll do it," Newboy said inside his head. "I'll eat, then we'll go." He stood and worked out some of the kinks. He wondered how long he'd slept. The whomping noise from above was insistent. He wouldn't have minded knowing what it was. He tended to be curious, even if he didn't show it. He pushed the board away from the window and pulled himself out into the night.

Broadway was ablaze with pulsating neon from one end to the other. Music blared from doorways: rock, opera, jazz, country, new age, hip-hop. The sidewalks were alive with shaved heads and hair that was spiked, Mohawked, plaited, set in cornrows, and dyed the colors of other planets' rainbows. Ears and lips and noses flashed with jewelry. Musicians played guitars and harmonicas and accordions and drums and spoons and violins. Knots of street kids, some younger than Newboy, huddled on corners, blowing into their hands, eyeing the passing world with exhausted wariness. The homeless were everywhere.

"Hey, little brother," somebody yelled at Newboy. "How you doing?"

Newboy unzipped his jacket.

"Are you willing to be saved?" a voice called out.

Stinko appeared.

"Video games," a voice yelled. "Upstairs to virtual reality."

"Coupons!" a man with red, white, and blue hair shouted. "Half off deli sandwiches with a coupon."

Newboy was looking for something he could afford.

He tried to push the hunger from his mind. He did his best to ignore the cold.

"What about Florida?" Stinko asked. "We could go there."

"I don't know anybody in Florida," Newboy said inside his head.

"You don't know anybody anywhere," Stinko said. "You liked the picture of Miami Beach you tore out of the magazine."

Newboy had removed the picture carefully from the magazine at the psychologist's office. He used it as a bookmark in his *Robinson Crusoe*.

"They have palm trees in Miami Beach," he said inside his head.

"So how do we get there?" Stinko asked. "Where is it?"

"It's a long way away," Newboy said inside his head. He was shoved violently from behind. He stumbled forward and tripped over his feet. He put his hands in front of him to break the fall. He felt a hard yank on his arm. The plastic bag was torn away. He chased the thief. But he hadn't seen a face. He hadn't seen anything. He had no idea who he was chasing. He gave up. Just like that his possessions were gone. He felt a pang about the book, then let it go.

"What are we going to do now?" Stinko asked. "They got everything."

"Not my money," Newboy said inside his head. "We're getting out of here. I've had enough of this place."

"Miami Beach," Stinko said.

"We'll find someplace closer," Newboy said inside his head as he pushed open the door of a taco stand. "Someplace easier to get to."

Stinko ordered the ninety-nine-cent special: rice, beans, bits of orange cheese, and shreds of lettuce that resembled packing material.

"You're a good-looking guy," the woman behind the counter said, flirting with Stinko. "Except for your nose and your ear and your eye."

"There's nothing wrong with me," Stinko said.

"I think you're cute," the counterwoman said. She batted her eyelashes. She smiled at Newboy. "You don't see them around much anymore," she said.

"I'm hungry," Stinko said. "May I please have my food now?"

"You're good," she said to Newboy. She gave him a jumbo cola on the house.

Newboy ate quickly. He left a twenty-cent tip. In the men's room he lined his sneakers with paper towels. He used the toilet, trying not to inhale the stench. He washed his face and hands. He went out into the night.

"Which way is Miami Beach?" Stinko asked.

"I don't know," Newboy said inside his head. He started walking.

"We'll keep going until it gets light," Stinko said. "Then we'll sleep. Then we'll go again. We'll keep doing it like that until we get there."

"Miami Beach is too far," Newboy said inside his head. He turned onto a side street. There were too many cops on Broadway.

"There was a big blue sky in that picture of Miami Beach," Stinko said. "There were pink birds with long legs called flamingos. There was a beach."

Newboy looked up as hard, raw rain began slapping him. The wind started pushing at his back. He passed an empty lot. A sheet of newspaper skittered across it like tumbleweed blowing through a ghost town.

"What difference does it make how far it is?" Stinko asked. "Look what's waiting for us when we get there."

Somebody cried out. Newboy stopped. It was nearby. He heard it a second time. It was a kid yelling for help.

"What are you waiting for?" Stinko asked.

"It's not my problem," Newboy said inside his head. Get involved, get in trouble. That was what he'd learned. He heard the kid yell again. It sounded bad.

"You have to help," Stinko said.

"I thought you wanted to get out of here," Newboy said inside his head.

"Help him," Stinko said.

"Nobody helps me," Newboy said inside his head.

"So what?" Stinko asked. "Do it."

Newboy heard the cry again. He removed his hand from Stinko's back, slid his left arm into its sleeve, zipped his jacket, and started running. He saw an alley. A hundred yards up it he saw two men hitting a kid. Their backs were to Newboy. They didn't hear him coming. He put his head down, charged into one of the men, and drove him into the wall of a building. The man screamed his surprise, then fell to the ground. The second man ran without looking to see what had happened. Newboy grabbed the kid's arm and pulled him to his feet. He was smaller than Newboy, a couple of years older. His eyes were as big and round as an owl's.

"Get back here!" the man Newboy had attacked yelled at his fleeing companion.

The kid took off down the alley, Newboy on his tail. "Faster!" the kid yelled. Newboy would have blown right past him if he'd known where he was going.

"There they are!" one of the men yelled.

They cut across the front yard of an old house, then along its side.

"Behind that house!" the other man yelled.

Newboy followed the kid into a scraggly woods. A moment later he found himself surrounded by decaying hulks of trees, and underbrush that was covered with mushrooms.

"Don't make a sound," the kid whispered.

For what seemed an eternity to Newboy, they stood as still as the trees that hid them.

"I'm not going in there," one of the men said from no more than twenty feet away.

"We'll find another one," the other man said.

The kid headed deeper into the woods. "Thanks for helping me," he said. "My name is Peeper. What's yours?"

Newboy decided not to reveal Stinko until he knew who this Peeper was and where they were going. He made sure Stinko was zipped in tight.

Peeper looked back. "Can't you talk?"

Newboy stopped.

"You need a place to stay?" Peeper asked.

Newboy looked past Peeper as his left eye began to wander.

"Come on," Peeper said.

Newboy hesitated. He and Stinko were supposed to be leaving the city tonight. But he was soaked to the skin and it was late to be starting a journey. He could put it off a few more hours.

"They call me Peeper because I can see in the dark," Peeper said. "Well, almost. I see a lot of things most people miss."

They reached the end of the woods and started down a hill, which the rain had turned as slippery as a greased cookie sheet. They went down it on their backsides, using their feet and hands as brakes.

Below him Newboy heard the hum of highway traffic. He saw a house. It was leaning away from him, like some sort of optical illusion. When he got closer, he saw that it had been knocked partway off its foundation. From mudslides, he guessed.

Peeper skirted the CONDEMNED sign in front of the house, then disappeared into a hole in the ground. Newboy took a deep breath and went in after him.

7 / A Place to Stay

Everything was out of kilter. Off center. Not at all the way it was supposed to be. It was like entering the fun house at an amusement park. The floor was tilted so severely that Newboy could hardly keep his footing. The house shifted a fraction of an inch, producing a moan that sounded almost human.

"Who's that with you, Peeper?" a kid's voice called out from the darkness ahead.

"He's all right," Peeper said. "He's a mute."

"Peeper's coming with a mute," the kid in the dark yelled up the stairwell.

Newboy could hear the murmur of voices from above as he started up the stairs behind Peeper. He wondered what he was getting himself into. Then all he could worry about was not falling backward. The house listed so badly that the staircase was like a wonky ladder. Peeper reached the top, leaving him to scale the last few steps alone. He thought about turning back.

"I can get past the kid at the bottom," he said inside his head. "Once I start running, nobody can catch me." He thought about getting out of the city right now, despite the hour.

A kid who was as tall as Newboy and fifty pounds heavier appeared above him. He was wearing a fedora and a ratty, once-elegant black overcoat that reached to the floor. His ears and lower lip were encrusted with silver rings. His fingers were covered with them. He reached out to give Newboy a hand.

Newboy rejected it.

The big kid grinned. "Peeper says you're all right," he said. He was three or four years older than Newboy. His face was pockmarked.

"He saved me from a beating," Peeper said. "Maybe worse."

Newboy reached the top and found himself in what had once been the living room. Scraps of discarded wood from construction sites burned in the fireplace, which was more like a pit. A dozen kids were scattered about, most of them sleeping in makeshift bedrolls, their hands clutching the bags that held what they owned. The rest eyed him with sleepy curiosity.

Newboy eyed them back. They were black and brown and tan and white. They were all different and all the same. He'd seen them, in some form or other, in his travels through the system. They'd run from foster homes or real homes or institutions where life was worse than it was on the streets. He looked for his stolen plastic bag.

There was no sign of it. The stale odor of urine and un-
washed bodies hung in the air.

"This is where we live right now," Peeper said. "We
call it the hotel. We're always moving." He flashed Newboy a smile. Peeper's nose was clotted with blood; his face
was a patchwork of welts.

"Peeper's okay," Newboy said inside his head. "He's a
lot like me."

"I'm Silverquick," the big kid said. "What's your
story?"

"I told you, he's a mute," Peeper said. "I'll get a pencil
and some paper in the morning. He can write it out for
us."

Peeper turned to Newboy. "You can write, can't
you?"

"I can do a lot of things," Newboy said inside his head.
"None of them are anybody's business unless I say so."

"Maybe he's deaf too," Silverquick said. "Maybe he's a
retard. I'm not having any retards."

"He's not a retard," Peeper said.

"Okay for tonight," Silverquick said. "I'll check him
out tomorrow." Silverquick moved to the fireplace, acting
like Newboy didn't matter until he said so.

Peeper led Newboy up another set of stairs, to a room
in the back of the house. The angle of the floor was so
steep that Newboy had to hold on to the wall to keep
from falling over.

"This is where I sleep," Peeper said. "It's quieter up
here. Take that corner. You won't slide."

Newboy took the corner across from Peeper. He watched Peeper shake out his blanket. He heard car tires slicing through the rain-slick surface of the highway. He heard the kids sleeping below.

"Don't worry about Silverquick," Peeper said. "He'll let you stay."

Newboy wasn't worried. He'd be out of there with the rising sun.

"He'll ask you where you're from and why you're running and what you've got on you," Peeper said. "We're all running, so that's easy. My old man used to beat my legs with a bicycle chain when he was having a bad day. You and me, we can hang out."

Newboy unzipped his jacket.

"We can watch each other's backs," Peeper said.

Stinko appeared. "My name is Stinko," he said.

"Stinko?" Peeper grinned at the sight of the doll. He looked at Newboy.

"Yeah, Stinko," Stinko said. "That a problem?"

"Not for me," Peeper said. He made his way to Newboy's corner. "I never met a Stinko before," he said. He studied the doll, then laughed.

"What's so funny?" Stinko demanded.

"You're funny," Peeper said. "We have to whisper. We don't want anybody hearing us. How come you waited until now to talk?"

"We had to be sure we could trust you," Stinko said.

"How do you know you can?" Peeper asked.

"Because I can tell," Stinko said.

"How come you don't talk by yourself?" Peeper asked Newboy.

"What difference does it make who does the talking?" Stinko asked back.

"No difference," Peeper said. "It's just not something you see every day. Where you from?"

"I ran away from a foster home," Stinko said. "Why were those men hitting you?"

"Some people like to beat up street kids," Peeper said. "I don't know why. Where was the foster home?"

"Out in Greenridge," Stinko said.

"I lived in a foster home near there once," Peeper said.

"Two Hundred and Eleventh Street," Stinko said.

"I was at a Hundred and Eighty-ninth," Peeper said. "Leicester Heights. You ever live on the streets before?"

"No," Stinko said.

"You have to watch out all the time," Peeper said. "Somebody's always trying to steal your stuff or hurt you. The cops are always looking for you."

"We're not staying here," Stinko said. "We're leaving in the morning."

"Where are you going?" Peeper asked.

"Miami Beach," Stinko said.

"It's too far," Newboy said inside his head.

"It is not too far," Stinko said.

"How come Miami Beach?" Peeper asked. "I never heard of it."

"The sun is always out in Miami Beach," Stinko said. "You can go swimming all the time."

"I'll come with you," Peeper said.

Newboy was amazed. He'd never considered the idea of company beyond Stinko. This was the first time he'd ever encountered anybody who wanted anything to do with him.

"Why?" Stinko asked.

"Because it's cold here," Peeper said, "and I hate the cold. I'm tired of what I'm doing. I don't like it. I've been thinking about going somewhere else. How do we get there?"

"We just go," Stinko said.

"How far is it?" Peeper asked.

"Too far," Newboy said inside his head. He didn't want to carry a bigger burden than he could handle. He just wanted a place to live.

"It's however far it is," Stinko said.

Newboy wondered why he kept arguing with himself.

"Maybe there's a place closer," Peeper said, "that's also warm."

"We'll go until we get there," Stinko said. "What could be easier than that?"

"Okay," Peeper said. "I'm in. We leave in the morning. Before the others get up."

Newboy removed the paper towels from his sneakers. They dripped cold water. He took off his socks and wrung them out.

"Want to share my blanket?" Peeper asked.

"Yes," Stinko said.

Newboy put his wet socks back on, then his sneakers.

He had to be ready to run. He got under the blanket, which was nearly stiff with filth.

"Thanks," Stinko said.

"As long as I have a blanket, you have a blanket," Peeper said.

8 / The Promise

A car pulled to the curb. The passenger door opened.
The woman behind the wheel smiled. It was his mother.
She was beautiful, as he'd imagined her. He started to get
in. His mother turned into the smiling, pie-faced Mrs.
Knox. He awoke with a start. He heard voices. They were
coming from inside the house. He shook Peeper.

"We have to get out of here," Stinko said.

Peeper was on his feet in an instant. He made his way
quickly up the floor's incline. "Move it," he said.

The voices grew louder. Newboy heard the stern com-
mands of adults.

"I'm coming," Stinko said.

Newboy zipped Stinko in tight and hurried up the
floor. He tripped on his feet and fell backward. He heard
yelling below. He heard squad car radios crackling in the
electrically charged air. He saw swirling ribbons of red
and blue light washing across the walls and ceiling.

"What are you doing?" Peeper asked, coming back to

get him. He pushed Newboy to a short set of steps, then up them to a small room on the top floor. Peeper kicked at the window. It popped out, frame and all.

"You always need a way out," he said.

Newboy peered through the hole where the window had been. He was looking straight down at the ground. His stomach started churning. Just looking made him dizzy. He thought he was going to be sick.

"Clear them all out!" a cop yelled.

"Leave me alone!" a kid screamed.

"Bend your knees when you hit the ground," Peeper said.

"I can't do it," Newboy said inside his head.

A cop moved into the doorway behind them. "Stop!" he yelled.

"I'll be right behind you," Peeper said. He pushed Newboy out.

Newboy fell like a rock from the sky. He saw the ground rushing toward him and remembered to bend his knees. He hit and rolled and came to a stop. He was alive. He unzipped his jacket and checked Stinko. It was hard to tell, but Stinko seemed no worse for the experience.

"Run!" Peeper shouted.

Newboy saw Peeper in the window. He saw flashlight beams headed his way.

"I'll look for you!" Peeper shouted.

"I'll look for you!" Stinko shouted back.

Newboy saw a cop clear the corner of the house. He

started running. His feet straightened out and he was gone. He ran parallel to the elevated highway, then underneath it into the forest of concrete pillars that held it up. He heard the crackle of damp wood being burned. He moved cautiously from pillar to pillar until he saw a gathering of homeless men warming themselves, staring into the flames. A tremor of fear shot through him.

He retraced his steps, then headed for high ground, out from beneath the highway, to the woods where he and Peeper had escaped the two men. He found a tangled cage of branches and crawled into the small opening at its center. He was protected here from the rain and wind. Nobody could see him, even if they walked right by.

"Peeper saved us," Stinko said.

"We're even," Newboy said inside his head.

"It doesn't work like that," Stinko said.

"I don't owe him anything," Newboy said inside his head.

"We're not going to Miami Beach without him," Stinko said.

"Who said we're going to Miami Beach?" Newboy said inside his head.

"We're not going anywhere without him," Stinko said.

"He got caught," Newboy said inside his head. "There's nothing I can do about it."

"Maybe he didn't get caught," Stinko said. "We didn't see him get caught. Maybe he got away. He said he'd look for us. We said we'd look for him."

"We can't take the chance," Newboy said inside his head. "The Knoxes will get me."

"Peeper could have jumped and let you get caught," Stinko said.

Newboy zipped his jacket.

"You made a promise," Stinko said, just before his head was covered and Newboy pulled his finger from the loop.

9 / Looking for Peeper

Newboy peered out through the branches at a morning veiled in mist. He couldn't see five feet in front of him. His neck ached. He was numb. He stretched and banged his body against the cage. A startled crow screamed its surprise and flapped away. Newboy saw his breath shooting out in front of him. He unzipped his jacket and put his finger into the loop.

"Good morning, Stinko," he said inside his head.

"Good morning, Newboy," Stinko said. "He could have jumped first and left you for the cops. He didn't have to help us."

"He owed me," Newboy said inside his head.

"Not everybody pays back," Stinko said.

Newboy left the thicket and made his way through the woods until he could see the leaning house where Peeper had brought him. It was encircled with yellow police tape. New CONDEMNED and NO TRESPASSING signs had been posted. The homeless men he'd seen under the highway the night before were moving in. A day ago he hadn't even known of Peeper's existence. He didn't want to get involved now. He had his own problems. He had to get going.

He cut back through the woods and found the alley where he'd first encountered Peeper. "I'm not going after him!" he yelled inside his head. "I don't care what he did."

"You are going after him," Stinko said. "He could be in trouble."

"I have to look out for myself," Newboy said inside his head. "I have to take care of me."

"You need him," Stinko said.

"I don't need anybody," Newboy said inside his head.

"You have a better chance of getting somewhere with Peeper," Stinko said.

Newboy heard an engine downshift behind him. He looked for a quick way out of the alley, but it was too late to run. Newboy stepped to the side. A pickup truck drove past. The driver eyed him. The truck stopped. A tall, gaunt man in work clothes stepped out.

Newboy started running.

"That jacket's no good in this weather," the man yelled after him. "Take mine."

Newboy looked back. The man took off his jacket and laid it on the ground.

"It's warmer," the man said.

Newboy waited until the truck was gone, then approached the jacket. "Why would somebody give me anything?" he asked inside his head.

"What do you care?" Stinko said. "Try it on."

Newboy poked at the leather jacket with his foot. He picked it up. It was heavy, frayed, worn at the elbows. It had a wool lining. He took his jacket off and put the new one on. It was too large, but it was warm and there was more room for Stinko. He zipped Stinko in, freed his arm from its new sleeve, and found the loop. He left his old jacket for whoever needed it.

"Let's go find Peeper," Stinko said.

Newboy checked Broadway. He checked the side streets off Broadway. He was aware of every police car. His brain took snapshots of a thousand faces, none of them Peeper's.

In the window of a tailor's shop he saw a clock. Mr. Knox was just dropping the boys off at school. After that he'd fetch his wife and they'd come looking for him.

He walked past Triphammer's Funeral Home, then past Mercy Hospital. He hooked up with Harrison Street, then Twenty-fifth, then found himself in Chinatown. He saw roasted ducks hanging in the windows of restaurants, and aquariums of fish and crabs, and bins of bok choy and ginger and water chestnuts. He passed noodle houses and dim sum parlors. He inhaled the sweet, sticky aroma of baking fortune cookies. He saw the pale eye of the sun through the haze of a milky sky.

He searched the train station. He circled the baseball

stadium. He moved on to Settlers Square, the original part of the city. He stopped to look through the window of a glass-blowing studio. He could see the heat of the furnace in the faces of the men and women who worked the molten glass in and out of the ovens. They were sweating. He searched along the docks of the riverfront.

10 / Close Encounters

Night dropped on the city. Newboy made his way back to the area around Broadway. He'd searched for Peeper where he'd found street people. He'd followed his feet until it pained him to walk.

"Have you seen Peeper?" Stinko asked until Newboy thought he'd go hoarse. Stinko described Peeper with all the detail Newboy could recall. Nobody had seen him. Nobody had heard of him.

Newboy made it the length of one side of Broadway. He was too cold to do more. His legs were cramped. His stomach howled. The faces he passed were out of focus. He could have walked right past Peeper without seeing him. He went into a mini-mart that was promoting day-old doughnuts, a dollar a dozen.

"I'll take six doughnuts for fifty cents," Stinko said.

"A dozen to a box," the small, happy man behind the cash register said. "I don't break them up."

"I can't eat a dozen doughnuts," Stinko said.

"Save some for tomorrow," the man said.

"Tomorrow they'll be hard as rocks," Stinko said.

"They're already hard as rocks," the man said.

"That's why I only want six," Stinko said.

"You can have the dozen for seventy-five cents," the man said. "You can't tell anybody."

"I won't even tell him," Stinko said, meaning Newboy.

The man smiled broadly. "You are very clever," he said to Newboy. "Take the dozen for fifty cents. It would be my pleasure."

Newboy headed for the boarded-up warehouse where he'd slept the day before. When the traffic light changed, he crossed Broadway. He was preoccupied with his mother, wondering where she might be at this very moment, wondering what she was doing. He didn't see the Knoxes' green van. He was speculating about the possibility that his mother had had other children, that he might come across a brother or sister someday. He didn't see Mr. Knox pointing at him, his mouth too full of ham and cheese to speak.

"Your mother left you to die," a foster parent had once told Newboy. He'd never believed it. His mother had been a street kid. He knew this in his heart. Her circumstances had been no better than his own.

Because he was preoccupied, he didn't see Mrs. Knox taking a bite out of her own sandwich while she studied the map of the city in her lap. He didn't see Mr. Knox poke his wife in the ribs to get her attention. He was gone when the van made a right turn from the left lane.

He didn't see Mrs. Knox whack Mr. Knox when they couldn't find him. He didn't see Mrs. Knox circle Broadway on her map.

Newboy pried the board loose and lowered himself into the basement. He removed the box of doughnuts from inside his jacket. He selected one from the middle, hoping it might be fresher. He took a bite. It was dry and old-tasting. He wished he had something to wash it down, like a gallon of hot chocolate. The whomping noise started upstairs.

"Let's go see what it is," Stinko said.

"No," Newboy said inside his head. "Forget it."

"Just a fast look," Stinko said.

"It's got nothing to do with you," Newboy said inside his head.

"Ah, come on," Stinko said. "A fast look."

"What's wrong with you?" Newboy asked inside his head. "We go up there, we get caught."

"It sounds like music," Stinko said.

"You must think I'm an idiot," Newboy said.

"It could be a band," Stinko said.

"It's people," Newboy said inside his head. "People are trouble."

"We'll sneak up on them," Stinko said. "They won't even know we're there. I want to see. I want to know what it is before I spend the night down here. Maybe it's a cult. Maybe we'll be murdered in our sleep."

"Okay," Newboy said inside his head, like he'd lost an argument. "Stop bugging me. We'll look." It made sense to know if he was in danger. He zipped up his jacket. He found the stairs and made his way to the first floor. He heard a train whistle in the distance. It sounded sad. Trains had always sounded sad to Newboy. The whomping sound grew louder.

The second floor was deserted like the first, as were the third and fourth, caverns of empty space. He reached the last flight of stairs. He could see light coming from beneath the door at the top. He made his way up the stairs until he reached that gap. The whomping sound coming from the other side filled his ears and made his head pulsate with the rhythm. He saw bare feet jumping up and down and sliding about to steel drum music.

What struck Newboy right away was that the feet were wrong. There was something the matter with them. They didn't look like feet. They didn't have skin on them. The feet weren't real.

The door opened with a hard pull, and Newboy fell halfway down the stairs. Framed above him was a square-shaped man in a baggy gray suit and white shirt. He had long white hair and was holding a ball-peen hammer in a raised hand.

"What do you want?" the dancing man's voice boomed.

"To dance," Newboy said inside his head. "I want to dance."

"Go away before I call the police," the dancing man said. "Go away!"

Newboy ran all the way to the basement. He grabbed

the doughnuts and pulled himself up and out into the night. He ran through the streets to the concrete pillars beneath the highway.

"That didn't work out so good," Stinko said when Newboy had regained his breath.

"You're the one who had to see what was going on," Newboy said. Out loud. In his own voice. Which came out of his own mouth.

"I talked," Newboy yelled. "I can talk by myself. I'm talking right now. I can hear myself. It's my voice coming out of my mouth going to my ears."

"Maybe the man with the hammer scared you into talking," Stinko said.

"He didn't look like he was going to use it," Newboy said.

"You can't always tell what people will do by the way they look," Stinko said.

"He can get around on those fake feet," Newboy said. "I wish I could dance."

"What's the point of dancing if you don't have some-where to do it?" Stinko asked.

"You can dance anywhere," Newboy said. He realized suddenly that he didn't need Stinko anymore. He could talk without him. But the thought of life without Stinko seemed impossible now. There would be an unfilled space inside his jacket. And what if he stopped talking again? He'd need Stinko then. Besides which, he didn't want to talk to anybody but Stinko. He didn't want any-body but Stinko to hear his voice. Stinko would keep talking to the rest of the world so he wouldn't have to. Stinko was company. Stinko wasn't going anywhere except with him.

"We'll find Peeper in the morning," Newboy said.

"Tomorrow is the day," Stinko said.

Newboy zipped Stinko in and retrieved a doughnut from the box.

"I can talk," he said, just to be sure he still could.

11 / Who's a Dummy?

The neglected three- and four-story buildings had once been the best in the city. Now they belonged to the poor, and to bars and pool halls and thrift stores and missions and other businesses that couldn't afford the rent elsewhere. There was a podiatrist's office with a papier-mâché foot over the door. The big toe was missing. Next to it was a free clinic. Next to that was a movie theater gone dark. A lot had gone dark in the neighborhood called Old Town.

Newboy had Stinko ask about Peeper. He looked and he listened. He learned nothing. He saw a group of street kids gathered by a low-slung building. He could hear one of them coughing.

"There are too many," Newboy said. "It could be dangerous."

"Don't get too close," Stinko said. "Something happens, we run. Stop thinking about it so much. Ask them."

Newboy realized that he'd started changing the sound of Stinko's voice. It was tougher than his own. It had attitude. He took a deep breath and crossed the street. He saw the kids watching him. They were dressed in ragtag layers of misfitting shoes and pants and shirts and sweaters and jackets and coats and scarves and hats and gloves. It looked like they were wearing everything they owned.

"It'll be all right," Stinko said.

"It had better be," Newboy said. He saw a kid who looked like an armored vehicle break free from the group.

"That's the boss," Stinko said.

"Why are they always so big?" Newboy asked.

"Big, but not so smart," Stinko said.

"We hope," Newboy said.

"Who are you?" the boss demanded.

Newboy saw the other kids moving in around him. He looked the boss in the eye and saw that he was in the presence of danger. Newboy's left eye started wandering, so that he appeared to be looking at two different things at once.

"My name is Stinko," Stinko said. "Who are you?"

"Smirk," the boss said.

"Sounds like gas," Stinko said.

"Stop it!" Newboy yelled inside his head. "You'll get us killed."

"I'm looking for Peeper," Stinko said.

Smirk closed a meaty hand around Stinko's head. "I'm going to crush you," he said.

"Get your fat hand off me," Stinko yelled. "I'm Peeper's friend."

Newboy took a step back, hoping Smirk would let go of Stinko.

Smirk released Stinko's head and grabbed his nose and pulled.

"Hey!" Stinko yelled. "That's my nose."

Newboy took another step back.

"Look what I got," Smirk said. He held up the quarter inch of Stinko's nose he'd ripped off, like it was some kind of trophy. His own nose was squashed up against his face.

"I know Peeper," a tiny kid wearing three different colored sweaters said. He stepped forward. He coughed. It was hard, a dry rasp. He placed himself between Newboy and Smirk.

"Where is Peeper?" Stinko asked.

"I haven't seen him," the kid who coughed said.

"I have to find Peeper," Stinko said. "Anybody know where he is?"

Smirk raised his fist to hit Newboy. The kid who coughed stayed between them.

"Leave him alone," the kid who coughed said. "A friend of Peeper's is okay."

Smirk gave the kid who coughed a long look. Then he grinned. "Sure, Hacker," he said. "Whatever you say, Hacker." He fixed a hard, steady gaze on Newboy.

"I see you or that talking doll again," he said, "I'll crush you both."

Newboy turned and walked off as casually as he could. He heard the kids laughing. He heard the kid called

Hacker coughing. He turned the corner, then crossed the street. He heard somebody padding along behind him. He glanced back. It was a girl. She was alone. She wore plaid pants and a black jacket. She was his age. He turned into an alley.

"Why can't you talk for yourself?" the girl asked, moving into the alley behind him. Her voice was as small as the rest of her. "It's a little freaky."

Newboy didn't want anything to do with her, whoever she was. So what if she was alone? So what if he didn't remember seeing her back there with Smirk? Even if she wasn't one of them, she wanted something.

"I can help you find Peeper," the girl said.

Newboy stopped.

"Here comes the dummy," she said.

"Who's a dummy?" Stinko asked.

"You're a dummy," she said.

"You don't look so smart yourself," Stinko said.

"A ventriloquist's dummy," she said, looking at Newboy. They were about ten feet apart. "I saw one on television. One of those old shows. Paul Winchell was the ventriloquist. Jerry Mahoney was the dummy. They were funny. You're not. Your mouth moves all the time."

"He can move his mouth all he wants," Stinko said. "Where's Peeper?"

"I didn't say I knew where he was," she said. "I said I could help you find him. I know where kids hide."

"Why do you want to help me?" Stinko asked.

"Because I'm trying to get away from Smirk," she said.

"I'm sure he's already looking for me." She moved past him up the alley. "We have to hurry."

In two steps he caught up to her. He watched her bite her fingernails.

"I'm Penny," she said. "What kind of name is Stinko?"

"You want to make something out of it?" Stinko asked.

"It's your name," she said. "What do I care?" She looked up at Newboy. "You've got me talking to the dummy."

"Then why are you looking at him?" Stinko asked.

"The one who makes you talk," she asked, her gaze swinging to Stinko, "what's his name?"

"Newboy," Stinko said.

"What's his last name?" she asked.

"He doesn't have one," Stinko said.

"Only famous people have one name," she said.

Newboy picked up his pace considerably. She made him apprehensive. She was a stranger, and a girl. He'd never spent time with girls. And he was still convinced she wanted something from him. She had to trot to keep up. She didn't seem to mind.

They spent the afternoon searching the Industrial District, which was the first place Penny thought Peeper might be. They searched empty buildings together, and beneath loading docks, and inside railroad containers. Once, when she was ahead of him, she stumbled and nearly fell, and he recognized how small and truly alone she was.

They searched until they ran out of light.

12 / Penny

"I know where we can sleep," Penny said.

"We have to keep looking for Peeper," Stinko said.

"I'm tired," she said. "I can't."

Newboy could see that she was exhausted. He felt it himself.

"Where will we look tomorrow?" Stinko asked.

"Near the college," she said. "Queen Street." She wrapped her jacket tightly around herself, folded her arms across her chest, and pushed off into the wind.

"Why do you want to find Peeper?" Stinko asked as Newboy followed the girl.

"He was good to me once," she said. "Maybe he'll help me get away."

Penny led them to a neighborhood called the Terrace, to a church that had once been a house. She moved to a side door and opened it by pressing her weight against it, lifting and jiggling the knob at the same time.

Newboy looked around to make sure nobody was watching, then stepped in after her. She closed the door and nudged the lock back into place. There was barely enough room for the two of them in the narrow space between the outer door and the inner door to the rest of the building. They sat on the floor facing each other, her back against one wall, his against the other.

"How do you know about this place?" Stinko asked.

"From another kid," Penny said. "I stayed here a few nights. Before Smirk got me. You can't get through the door to the inside. We have to leave before it gets light."

In her wavering voice, Newboy could hear her shivering. He set Stinko and the doughnuts on his lap, took off his jacket, and held it out to her.

"I don't need it," she said.

"I was getting hot anyway," Stinko said. "Take it."

She put it on over her jacket. The sleeves dangled six inches below her fingers. She pulled the bottom of it over her knees.

"You're goofy-looking," she said.

"Who you calling goofy-looking?" Stinko asked.

"The other one," she said. "Newboy. He looks goofy."

"That's not his fault," Stinko said.

"You look goofy too," she said. "Not that it matters. Looks are the least important thing."

Newboy handed her a doughnut.

"Eat it in small bites," Stinko said.

Newboy bit off part of his. He could barely chew it.

"Why didn't you run away from Smirk before?" Stinko asked.

"I did," she said. "He hurt me when he caught me. I was afraid after that. Until I saw you. If Smirk didn't tear you apart, you were the one."

"I was going to tear Smirk apart," Stinko said.

"Hacker saved you," she said. "He's kind of Smirk's good-luck charm. He's the only one who can talk back and get away with it."

"How can Peeper help you?" Stinko asked.

"He has good ideas," she said.

"About what?" Stinko asked.

"About where I could go," she said. "About what I could do. I can't stay here. I can't go home. Maybe Peeper could think of something. Why are you looking for him?"

Newboy had Stinko tell Penny how he'd saved Peeper and how Peeper had saved him. He didn't say anything about them going off together. He didn't want anybody else tagging along.

"How come you can't go home?" Stinko asked when he was done.

"None of your business," she said. "Why are you running?"

"None of your business," Stinko said. "How long have you lived on the streets?"

"Five months," she said. "Who you running from?"

"You ever been in the state system?" Stinko asked.

"No," she said.

"I've been in it my whole life," Stinko said. "That's how come I'm running. How do you live on the streets? How do you survive?"

"You beg when you have to," she said. "You steal when you're hungry. You get somebody to protect you. You take favors and pay back what they want. The state system can't be worse than that."

"You're in jail in the state system," Stinko said.

"You're in hell on the streets," she said.

"Why can't you go home?" Stinko asked.

"The same reason you can't go back to the system," she said.

"Then go someplace else," Stinko said.

"Everywhere is the same," she said. "If you're a street kid they spit at you. They beat you up. They do worse than that."

"Not everybody," Stinko said.

"Everybody," she said.

"There has to be a better place than this," Stinko insisted. "Where do you come from?"

"Where do you come from?" she replied.

"I don't know," Stinko said.

Newboy took another bite of his doughnut.

"This is like eating a rock," she said, chewing on hers. "Don't you have any family?"

"Nobody," Stinko said. "So what?"

"So nothing," she said. "You're lucky."

"How can I be lucky if I don't have a family?" Stinko asked.

"I wish I didn't have any," she said.

"You have a mother?" Stinko asked. "A father?"

"A drunk father," she said.

"Better than no father," Stinko said.

"No it isn't," she said. "This doughnut is made out of cardboard."

"More like wood," Stinko said.

It didn't occur to Newboy that he was making Stinko's mouth move even though he didn't have to. It was dark. She couldn't see him doing it. He could have talked in Stinko's voice and she wouldn't have known the difference. But each time he had a question, each time he had something to say, he pulled on the loop. It had become second nature.

"I'm from Squamish Falls," she said after they'd gnawed on their doughnuts in silence for a while.

"Where's that?" Stinko asked.

"Up north a few hundred miles," she said.

"That's where your father is?" Stinko asked.

"My father comes after me when he's drinking," she said. "When my sister is older, he'll go after her."

"You have a sister?" Stinko asked.

"I just said so, didn't I?"

"How old is she?"

"Eight."

"You have an eight-year-old sister?"

"You deaf?"

"Who takes care of her?"

"She's smart," Penny said. "There are people who keep an eye on her."

"Where's your mother?"

"Who knows?"

"Then you have to do it," Stinko said.

"Do what?" Penny asked.

"Take care of your sister," Stinko said.

"Nobody did it for me," Penny said.

"You still have to do it," Stinko said.

Newboy swallowed the last of his doughnut. He had Stinko tell Penny about the foster homes he'd lived in, lumping them together so it came out like one story instead of eleven. He spoke in a whisper because he knew she was sleeping. He could hear her breathing. He could hear her heart beating. It fluttered like a bird's.

He discovered that he liked talking about his life if nobody was listening. He was saturated with the past. He needed to empty himself so there would be room for the future. He talked on through the night, working Stinko's mouth and talking in Stinko's voice. He talked until it was time to go.

13 / Going Home

Newboy watched Penny wake up. Her eyes blinked like she didn't know where she was. She looked at Newboy, then Stinko, with alarm.

"We're going to the bus station," Stinko said. Newboy had decided this in the early hours of the morning. When he'd stopped talking long enough to force another doughnut down his gullet.

"You're going to take care of your sister," Stinko said. "I'll buy the ticket. If I don't have enough money, I'll find a way to get more."

Penny shook off the final haze of sleep. Her expression hardened.

A spasm of pain shot through Newboy's right leg. It was locked in a cramp from being bent all night. His right foot was all pins and needles.

"I'm not going," she said.

He stood and stamped his foot on the floor.

"You have to see if she's okay," Stinko said.

"She's okay," Penny said.

"You have to see for yourself," Stinko said.

Penny opened the door and stepped outside.

"I need my jacket," Stinko said.

She took it off and handed it to Newboy, who zipped Stinko in and found the loop again.

"You have to be sure," Stinko said.

Newboy left the doughnuts. He never wanted to see another one.

"If your sister is okay, you can take off again," Stinko said. "But if she needs you, you have to stay. You're all she has."

"You can't tell me what to do," Penny said.

"Your sister needs you," Stinko said. "Someday you may need her."

Penny walked off.

"Do you like your sister?" Stinko asked as Newboy kept pace.

"She laughs like a horse," Penny said.

"What's her name?" Stinko asked.

"Mary," Penny said. "Sometimes I like her." She shrugged her shoulders, giving in. "I'll go see how she is."

The bus station seemed lonely to Newboy. It was dimly lit. There was only one window open for business.

"How much is a one-way ticket to Squamish Falls?" Stinko asked the agent, who had a horseshoe of frizzy red hair rimming his shiny head.

"Is it for you?" the agent asked, his smile growing.

"Who else?" Stinko responded. "And I get half off because I'm a kid."

"How old are you?" the agent asked.

"Twelve," Stinko said.

"You should be in school," the agent said. "You a runaway?"

"I'm off school this week," Stinko said. "I'm going to Squamish Falls to get a new nose, a new ear, and a new eye."

"You going into show business?" the agent asked Newboy.

"I do the talking," Stinko said. "Me. The one in front of you."

"You're not bad for a kid," the agent said to Newboy. "You don't see a lot of ventriloquists."

"So how much?" Stinko asked.

"There's no half fare," the agent said, "but you're in luck. We're having a sale this month. You can get there for twenty-two dollars and thirty-seven cents. The dummy can go for nothing."

"I don't like being called a dummy," Stinko said.

Newboy put a ten, a five, and eight singles on the counter.

"I have to go to the bathroom," Penny said when he handed her the ticket.

"I must be nuts spending all my money on her," Newboy said to Stinko while they were waiting. "I'm an idiot."

"You are an idiot," Stinko said.

"People are supposed to look out for themselves," Newboy said.

"That's how it is," Stinko said.

"Why should I care what happens to her or her sister?" Newboy asked. He saw a cop stroll in through the far door. He looked for a place to get out of sight. He could make it out the side door, but Penny would return while he was gone. She might change her mind and take off. She might get caught. He watched the cop coming slowly toward him. He hurried back to the ticket agent.

"I forgot to ask how long it takes to get to Squamish Falls," Stinko said. "I need to know how many magazines to buy."

"What do you read," the agent asked, "the dummy news? Let me look that up for you."

"I'm not a dummy," Stinko said.

The agent winked at Newboy. "Five hours and forty minutes," the agent said, "if it's on time."

Newboy heard the cop's shoes creaking up behind him.

"Get a load of this," the agent said to the cop. He pointed at Stinko.

The cop scrutinized Stinko, then Newboy.

"Say something," the agent said to Stinko.

"You're under arrest," Stinko said to the cop.

"Pretty good," the cop said.

"For impersonating a policeman," Stinko said.

The cop laughed.

"I'm on my way to Squamish Falls to get a new nose, a

new ear, and a new eye," Stinko said. "I'm going to be a movie star."

"He's off from school this week," the agent said to the cop. "A guy up there fixes dummies."

"He needs it," the cop said, shifting his slow gaze to Stinko.

"You don't look so hot yourself," Stinko said.

"Don't mouth off to a cop," Newboy said inside his head. "I'm trying to stay out of trouble here."

The cop started to say something, then saw a homeless man sleeping on a bench and headed for him. Newboy watched the cop hustle the man to the street. He saw Penny coming out of the ladies' room. He took her to the bank of vending machines, which dispensed soft drinks and hot coffee and sandwiches and candy. He put three quarters into the candy machine.

"Pick what you want," Stinko said.

She studied the contents, then pressed a button. The machine whirred. A small box of chocolate-covered caramels fell into the tray with a thunk.

"Take this," Stinko said.

Newboy handed her his last dollar bill.

She stuffed it into a pocket with the candy. They went to the platform. The bus had just arrived. Three passengers got off and collected their belongings.

"I'll tell Peeper where you are," Stinko said.

"If you find him," she said.

"I'll find him," Stinko said.

"How am I supposed to help my sister?" she asked.

"However you can," Stinko said.

"My father will come after me," she said.

"I don't know what you can do," Stinko said. "Maybe you can find somebody to stop him. You can't leave her alone."

Newboy could tell Penny was frightened. A hard wind would break her in half, he thought. That's how fragile she was. How could she stand up to a drunk father and protect her sister? That's what he was telling her to do. What if he was wrong?

The announcement to board for Kerry and Bend and Summermill and Golden and Squamish Falls and points north brought knots to both their stomachs.

"I'm afraid," she said.

So am I, Newboy thought.

"You'll be all right," Stinko said.

"How do you know?" she asked.

"You just will be," Stinko said.

"I'm going to make sure my sister is okay," Penny said, "then I'm leaving."

"Make sure before you go," Stinko said.

"You're a dummy," she said. She climbed into the bus.

"Takes one to know one," Stinko said.

Newboy watched as she made her way to a seat. She wouldn't look at him. When the bus pulled out, she held up her hand and moved it slowly back and forth. Newboy lifted his right hand into the air.

"We're broke," Stinko said. "We have five cents. You can't get anything for five cents."

"I'm zipping you up and looking for Peeper," Newboy said. He and Stinko were alone on the platform.

"You can zip me up all you want," Stinko said, "you still won't have any money."

"I can get along without money," Newboy said.

"I can get along without money," Stinko said. "You can't. How are you going to eat? What about Miami Beach?"

"Forget Miami Beach," Newboy said. "I want to find Peeper and get out of here."

A bus pulled in and unloaded its passengers.

"Let's go," Newboy said inside his head, not wanting to be heard by anybody passing by.

"We're not going anywhere without money," Stinko said. "You can get arrested for not having money."

"I'm not begging," Newboy said inside his head. "I'm not stealing."

A heavyset woman in an orange caftan, pulling an orange suitcase on wheels, put something in Newboy's hand. She looked like a harvest moon.

Newboy stared at the dollar bill. It was folded into the shape of a bird.

"What's it for?" Stinko yelled after the woman.

"I always give something to street performers," she said.

14 / The Street Performer

"All we did was talk," Newboy said inside his head.

"I'm the one she heard," Stinko said. "I'm why she gave us the money."

"She must have thought we were hard up," Newboy said inside his head.

"We are hard up," Stinko said.

"She called us street performers," Newboy said inside his head. "She gave us money and we didn't have to ask." He unfolded the bird to make sure the dollar was real.

"Money for talking," Stinko said.

Newboy walked quickly to Broadway. He kept an eye peeled for Peeper, the cops, and the Knoxes. He knew he was close to running out of time. The taco stand still had the ninety-nine-cent special. The woman waiting on him was new. She barely paid attention to either of them.

"How do I get to Queen Street?" Stinko asked when Newboy finished eating.

"Go left out the door and down the hill," the woman said, her eyes glued to the morning's tabloid.

Newboy took his last six cents out of his pocket. It wasn't going to do him any good. He put the coins on the counter next to his plate. He was down to nothing now. Zeroed out. Pretty much the way he'd been when he'd started life.

As he left Broadway, the Knoxes' green van turned onto it. If Mr. Knox hadn't spilled his spillproof container of tea on the floor, causing Mrs. Knox to swerve, they would have seen him. If Newboy had glanced back, he would have seen the van careening through a red light.

Queen Street was a smaller version of Broadway. It bordered the college on one side and serviced its population with a variety of cheap restaurants, coffeehouses, newsstands, music stores, movie theaters, video game parlors, and bookstores, used and new. Newboy's ears were flooded with music. His nostrils were invaded with the fragrance of pizza, then pierogi, then pho. He was hungry, despite just having eaten. He was always hungry. He couldn't ever remember feeling full. There were street musicians everywhere. A bearded man dressed like a Viking played the violin. A girl with red hair and freckles sat on the sidewalk, a boom box in her lap, while her twin brother clog-danced. An old woman with no teeth played blues on the harmonica.

Newboy took note of the shoe boxes and cigar boxes and the multitude of hats that the performers had set in front of them. He noted the bills and coins they contained. He covered one side of Queen Street, then made his way back down the other. No Peeper. He looked for a place to get warm.

He went into a shoe store and was escorted out. He was thrown out of a music store. If he'd had money he could have bought something to eat. He could have stayed as long as he pleased over a bowl of soup and mug of hot chocolate. A few dollars would have done it. He looked for a place to perform with Stinko. He passed a bookstore, then stepped back to watch a man inside reading to a dozen empty folding chairs. The man saw Newboy and waved him in.

"Sit anywhere," the man said when Newboy closed the door. He picked up where he'd left off.

Newboy sat in the chair nearest the heating vent. He felt himself begin to thaw. He tried to understand what the writer was reading. It seemed to be about the unlikely friendship between a dog and a dolphin. When the writer was done, he asked if there were questions.

"Why were you reading when nobody was here?" Stinko asked.

The writer gave Stinko a long look, then shifted his attention to Newboy. "In case somebody came by," he said.

"We came by," Stinko said.

"Sometimes it happens," the writer said. "Thank you for listening."

"I hope somebody buys your book," Stinko said.

"Me too," the writer said.

Newboy left his seat by the heating vent reluctantly. He opened the door to leave. The bell above it jingled.

"There's something you should know," the writer said.

Newboy looked back.

"Hope is the soap that floats in the bathtub of life," the writer said. "You'll make it."

Newboy set himself up outside the bookstore. Nobody was performing nearby. He placed a discarded coffee container on the sidewalk.

"We'll do some talking and make some money," Stinko said.

"You'll do some talking and I'll make some money," Newboy said inside his head. He turned his back to the street for dramatic effect. He could see the writer sitting at a table with a stack of his books, waiting. He spun around.

"My name is Stinko," Stinko yelled. "I said Stinko. Stinko is my name."

Somebody laughed. A few people stopped to see what was happening.

"I'm from outer space," Stinko said. "I'm from another planet. It's not far from here. Just on the other side of the sun."

Newboy flashed on Harpo Marx honking his horn. He was doing it. They were paying attention.

"It's called Harpo," Stinko said. "The planet I live on. I'm the smartest one there."

"You must be the only one there," somebody yelled.

"Okay, I'm not the smartest one," Stinko said. "I'm the best-looking."

That got a laugh. A few more people gathered. Somebody put a quarter in the coffee container. Newboy studied the faces around him.

"Okay, I'm not the best-looking one on Harpo," Stinko said.

"You're not the best-looking one anywhere," somebody yelled.

"You don't like the way I look?" Stinko asked the heckler. "So I'm missing an ear. So I can't get one of my eyes open. So part of my nose is gone. So what? Who's perfect?"

More laughter. More money in the cup.

"Has anybody seen Peeper?" Stinko asked. "I'm looking for Peeper."

"So am I," a voice said directly into Newboy's ear.

15 / The Deal Meal

"I'll have the meat loaf," Stinko said as Newboy closed the menu. "With the mashed potatoes and the peas and the gravy. Extra gravy. And a big hot chocolate. I'll order dessert later."

Newboy was sitting at a table in a restaurant across from Silverquick.

"Very good," the waiter said, like taking an order from a ventriloquist's dummy was a regular thing.

"Coffee," Silverquick said. "Cream and sugar."

"Oh, excellent choice, sir," the waiter said, making no effort to conceal his sarcasm. "We especially enjoy selling a cup of coffee at the height of dinner hour."

"Happy to help out," Silverquick said, flashing a smile that had all the warmth of a rubber stamp.

"How come you're feeding me?" Stinko asked when the waiter was gone.

"No friend of mine goes hungry," Silverquick said.

"I'm not your friend," Stinko said.

"I'm basing this on Peeper," Silverquick said. He leaned toward Newboy until he was halfway across the table. "You helped him. That makes the difference. That makes you my friend."

He jabbed a finger at Stinko's face. "What's with the doll?" he asked. "How come he talks and you don't?"

"Where is Peeper?" Stinko asked.

"I haven't seen him since the other night when the cops came," Silverquick said, leaning back. "How'd you get away?"

"Peeper got me out the window," Stinko said. "I don't know if Peeper made it."

"Even if they caught him, he got away by now," Silverquick said. "Peeper is resourceful. We'll find him together. What's your story?"

"My story is none of your business," Stinko said.

"You hurt me when you talk like that," Silverquick said.

The waiter brought the coffee. "Refills are a dollar," he said. He set milk and sugar on the table.

"Is the milk fresh?" Silverquick asked.

"We have a cow in the kitchen," the waiter said. "If it's not fresh enough, I'll send her out."

"You're going to get a big tip for being so funny," Silverquick said.

"I'll hurry it right over to the bank," the waiter said. He turned to Stinko. "Your meat loaf will be here momentarily."

Silverquick poured milk into his coffee, then added six packets of sugar. "I'm fifteen," he said when he'd stirred the mixture. "I've been on the streets since I was eleven. Since my father decided one day to use me for a football. I've been across the country on a freight train. I've been to jail. That's my story."

Newboy noticed that Silverquick's teeth were brown.

"I have to know your story," Silverquick said, "or I can't trust you. If I can't trust you, I can't help you find Peeper."

Newboy had Stinko tell Silverquick about running away from the Knoxes, without revealing their names or where they lived. He had to tell him something because he needed help. He'd lost confidence in his ability to find Peeper on his own.

His food arrived. His right hand shook with anticipation as he raised a forkful of meat loaf to his mouth. He closed his lips around it, slid the meat loaf free, chewed, and swallowed. It tasted like all the good things he'd imagined were possible in life.

Silverquick sipped his coffee. He added two more packets of sugar. "I worry about Peeper being out there," he said. "I want him back. I take care of my boys. I keep them safe. I find them places to sleep. I make sure they have what they need. Peeper should have shown me more thanks. But that's okay. I don't do it for the thanks. Finding him should only take a couple of days with all of us looking."

"I don't have a couple of days," Stinko said when New-boy's mouth was briefly free of food.

"What's the hurry?" Silverquick asked.

"The people I ran away from will catch me if I hang around too long," Stinko said.

"Don't worry about them," Silverquick said. "I protect my boys. You and me are going into business. What you did on Queen Street you can do better on Broadway. At night. More people. More money."

Silverquick emptied a pocket and set a handful of coins in front of Newboy. "I got this out of your cup," he said. "A buck fifty, tops."

Newboy put his fork down, scooped up the money, put it in his pocket, picked up his fork, and resumed eating.

"I'll find a spot," Silverquick said. "I'll make sure no-body bothers you. Including the cops. I'll have my boys look for Peeper. We'll split what you make, fifty-fifty."

"I can do it alone and keep all the money," Stinko said.

"I just want to help," Silverquick said, stirring another packet of sugar into his coffee. "With me you'll be safe. With me you'll find Peeper. You don't get something for nothing in this world. You make some, I make some, we're both happy."

After two more orders of meat loaf, mashed potatoes, and peas, plus two more hot chocolates and two wedges of coconut cream pie, Stinko belched Newboy's satisfaction.

"I'm full," Stinko said.

"You sure?" Silverquick asked. His expression had turned grim watching Newboy pack it away. "You could order a horse or something."

"I don't eat horses," Stinko said.

"What about an elephant?" Silverquick said. "On a bun. With the works."

"You said to have what I wanted," Stinko said.

"I like my boys to eat," Silverquick said.

"I'm not your boy," Stinko said.

Silverquick paid the bill. He left the waiter nothing. "That'll teach him to get smart with me," he said as he moved to the sidewalk.

Newboy and Stinko stayed just inside the open door.

"You got to trust me if we're going to be partners," Silverquick said.

"Who said we're partners?" Stinko asked.

"I bought you dinner," Silverquick said.

"You said there was no catch," Stinko said.

"Who said there's a catch?" Silverquick asked.

"There is if I have to be your partner because you bought me dinner," Stinko said.

"It was three dinners," Silverquick said. "And there's always a catch. That's how it works. You pay me back with one night on Broadway and we'll see what happens."

"Close the door," a customer yelled.

"You want to look for Peeper on your own, be my guest," Silverquick said. "You want help, I'm your man."

"Close the door," another customer yelled.

"Close it yourself," Silverquick yelled back, walking away.

"Okay," Stinko said as Newboy followed, pulling the door shut behind him. "One night."

16 / Life on Planet Stinko

"My name is Stinko," Stinko announced. **"That's my** name. Stinko."

A girl wearing white makeup and a long red dress came right up to Stinko and stared him in the face.

"Stand back!" Stinko shouted. "Give me room to breathe."

The girl stuck her tongue out and walked away. A man carrying a dog in a shoulder bag stopped to gawk.

"Hey," Stinko said to the dog, "you a dummy too?"

The dog barked.

Stinko snarled.

The man hurried off.

Newboy was in front of the Blue Moon Café, which was bathed in blue spotlights. It was where Silverquick had put him. A cigar box was on the sidewalk. Newboy looked around. He couldn't see Silverquick anywhere.

"That's right," Stinko shouted. "You heard me. My name is Stinko. I'm from the planet Harpo. I'm the only one on Harpo who can talk. The other guy on Harpo says nothing."

"Maybe you should shut up too," somebody yelled.

"I'm the best-looking one on Harpo," Stinko said. "I'm the smartest one on Harpo."

"The other one must be pretty stupid," the heckler yelled.

"He's a genius compared to you," Stinko said.

"The other one must be real ugly," somebody else said.

"So I'm missing an ear," Stinko said. "So I can't get one eye open. So part of my nose is gone. So what? Anyway, there isn't anybody on Harpo but me, so I'm the best-looking and the ugliest."

People started putting money in the cigar box.

"That's why I came here," Stinko said. "I'm looking for somebody to bring back with me."

"You stink, Stinko," a kid with hair that came to a point above his head shouted.

"Not as bad as you," Stinko shouted back.

"How'd you like to get your face pulled off?" the kid shouted, rushing forward to do Stinko damage.

From nowhere Silverquick flashed in front of Newboy. Just like that, the kid with the pointy hair was gone. Like magic. Just as suddenly, Silverquick's boys began to appear.

"There's nothing wrong with my nose that can't be fixed with Krazy Glue," Stinko said.

Newboy saw one of the boys move behind a woman,

stick his hand inside her purse, and remove her wallet. Then the boy was gone. Like magic.

"It's lonely on the planet Harpo," Stinko said. "Being the only one."

Newboy saw another boy lift a wallet from a man's pocket. He was losing his concentration. Silverquick was using Stinko to help him steal.

"Nobody takes stuff that doesn't belong to them on Harpo," Stinko said. "I took something once. It made me feel bad."

The crowd was waiting for the punch line.

"I picked my own pocket once," Stinko said. "That's how I found out I didn't have anything."

Some laughter. Not much.

Newboy saw one of the boys dipping into an old man's canvas bag.

"On Harpo we don't take things out of old people's bags," Stinko said.

Newboy saw Silverquick out of the corner of his eye. There was fury in his expression. He looked for a way to run. He was blocked in by Silverquick's boys, and the crowd. He heard a screech of tires. He saw a flash of green.

"Out of my way!" Mrs. Knox screamed as she leaped from the van. "Out of my way!" She pushed through the crowd toward Newboy.

Newboy's feet felt stuck to the ground, like they each weighed a million pounds.

"That's him!" Mrs. Knox screamed, knocking a man down.

Mr. Knox made his way along the edge of the crowd to Newboy's right, moving closer with each unobserved step.

"I've got you now," Mrs. Knox said as she reached for Newboy.

Silverquick cut her off.

Newboy pried his feet loose and started running. He saw Mr. Knox and reversed direction.

Silverquick spun Mrs. Knox around. "Beat it," he said, "before something bad happens."

Newboy hit full stride.

"Get him!" Mrs. Knox screamed at her husband as she struggled with Silverquick.

Silverquick turned to see who she was yelling about and saw Newboy.

"Come back here," he yelled. He let go of Mrs. Knox to give chase.

Mrs. Knox delivered a punch to Silverquick's midsection that turned his knees to jelly.

Newboy put Broadway behind him with all the speed he could muster. He ran full-out until he reached the woods. He crawled into his cage of branches and waited for his heart to catch up with him.

"We lost them," Stinko said.

"They'll be coming soon," Newboy said.

"I thought she had us back there," Stinko said.

"She almost did," Newboy said. He could still see her reaching for him, the twinkle of triumph in her eyes.

"We have to get out of here tonight," he said.

"What about Peeper?" Stinko asked.

"We're not going to find him," Newboy said.

"How do we know if we don't keep looking?" Stinko asked.

"You saw her," Newboy said. "You want her to get us? You want Silverquick to get us?"

"You want Silverquick to get Peeper?" Stinko asked.

"Peeper can take care of himself," Newboy said.

"One more day," Stinko said.

17 / One More Day

Newboy made his way through the city's west side.
He stuck to its quieter passageways. The narrow, littered
streets were lined with run-down cinder-block buildings
that were covered with graffiti. Every pane of glass in
them was broken. The empty lots were knee-high with
discarded rubbish. Newboy heard the blare of a boat's
horn—one long, one short—the signal to open the drawbridge he and Stinko had crossed an hour ago.

"There are too many places to hide here," Newboy
said.

"Just keep looking," Stinko said.

"He could be anywhere," Newboy said. "It's a waste of
time."

"He could be around the corner," Stinko said.

"He could be a hundred miles away," Newboy said.

"Why don't we go to the corner and look?" Stinko said.

Newboy went to the corner. A bus passed. Then a
truck.

"Let's try the next corner," Stinko said.

It took half a day to crisscross the streets of the west side. It took half an hour for Newboy to realize that he had to get out of the residential area next to it. The houses were small. They sat on small plots of land. They all had bars on the windows. He saw fearful faces watching him. He knew somebody would call the police. Peeper would never be here.

Newboy walked on streets that were unfamiliar to him, that took him through a neighborhood of large houses with large porches and large yards, with large signs announcing that they were under the protective care of a private security force. He saw a small white car with a red bubble light on top coming toward him. He returned to the river and crossed the bridge and headed downtown.

The bright lights and glitter of downtown's Avenue of Dreams dazzled Newboy. He could barely believe what was in the windows of stores: clothes from Europe, cameras, furniture, shoes, luggage, leather goods, stationery, cookware, motor scooters, toys. Doormen who looked like generals stood at attention in front of hotels. Thousands of tiny white lights winked on and off from the branches of trees and arms of lampposts.

The street was crowded with shoppers and cops. Newboy turned down a side street, then into an alley. He stopped for a moment by the open kitchen door of an Italian restaurant to inhale garlic cooking in olive oil and spicy sausages and tomato sauce. He heard yelling and saw two men fighting over a paper bag. He hurried now.

He heard footsteps and looked back, just in time to see the length of pipe that hit him on the head.

The force of the blow knocked him to his knees. The world began to spin like he was trapped inside a clothes dryer. He fell the rest of the way to the ground. His eyes locked shut. Passing footsteps sounded like hands clapping. Car horns sounded like trumpets. The voice of whoever was pulling at him sounded like rushing water.

When his head began to clear, Newboy pushed himself to his feet. His knees buckled and he fell. He tried a second time, then a third, then made it. His head throbbed. He touched the spot where he'd been hit. A lump like an egg was rising. He felt for Stinko. His jacket was empty. Stinko was gone. Stolen. He was certain he knew who'd done it. Silverquick was getting back at him for running. He pulled himself together and started for Broadway, determined to rescue yet another lost friend.

Silverquick was nowhere to be found. Neither were any of his boys. Newboy looked until he lost the strength to continue. He needed sleep and warmth. His head felt like it was being tightened in a vise. He returned to the abandoned warehouse. He lowered himself into the basement. He heard the whomping noise coming from the top floor. He wouldn't bother the dancing man, the dancing man wouldn't bother him.

18 / The Dancing Lesson

Newboy was in Miami Beach. He could smell the ocean. He could feel the sand between his toes. He could feel his body baking in the sun, the hot, beautiful sun. Which kept getting closer. And closer. Until it was shining in his eyes.

"You're the boy with the dummy," the voice behind the flashlight said.

Newboy had heard the voice. It belonged to the dancing man.

"The dummy's name was Stinko," the dancing man said. "I saw you on Broadway. You were entertaining, while it lasted. Why did that lady attack you?"

Newboy started inching his way toward the window.

"You can go if you like," the dancing man said. He lowered the ball-peen hammer he was holding. "I'm not going to call the police."

Newboy tripped over his feet, fell, and jumped up.

"Are you all right?" the dancing man asked.

Newboy's hand reached for the window. He was almost there.

"You can sleep down here," the dancing man said. "This isn't the first time we've met, after all. It's not as though I don't know who you are. And I have seen you perform." He lowered the flashlight so Newboy could see him.

Newboy hesitated.

"You could join me for dinner, if you like," the dancing man said. "I was just fixing myself something when I decided to come down. I do that several times a night since I discovered you outside my door. That gave me a fright. I can't get anybody to come fix the window. You can't get anybody to do anything these days."

"Why shouldn't I get something to eat?" Newboy asked inside his head. "It's dangerous out there, it's dangerous in here. At least in here I won't be hungry."

He followed the dancing man upstairs. He passed through the door he'd peeked under, into a room the size of a basketball court. At one end were chairs and tables and shelves filled with books and recessed windows the size of doors. In the middle was the kitchen. Most of the rest was dance floor.

"Wash up," the dancing man said, throwing Newboy a towel. "Use all the hot water you want." He pointed to the kitchen sink.

Newboy took off his jacket, rolled up his sleeves, opened the hot water spigot to full bore, and stuck his head under the goosenecked faucet. He washed his hair and neck and face and hands and arms.

"You're a street child," the dancing man said. "I don't want to know why. Everybody has a story." He was working at the stove and oven, putting the finishing touches on dinner.

"You're heading out in search of the future," the dancing man said. "It's a dicey business. You have to wrap your arms around what you don't know yet, or you'll miss the chance. What's your name?"

Newboy didn't respond.

"I don't have one either," the dancing man said. "I gave it up when words started losing their meaning."

Newboy dried his head.

The dancing man poured two glasses of fizzy water from a yellow bottle.

"I've seen a whale break free of the ocean like it was trying to fly," the dancing man said. "I've spent a whole day watching gorillas taking care of each other. I've seen herds of animals on the run in Africa that were so large they made the ground shake for a hundred miles. I've seen a baby elephant napping in the shade of its mother's stomach. I've seen a baby wildebeest take its first step."

He handed Newboy his glass. "Fancy seltzer," he said. "Two cents plain for two bucks."

Newboy took a long drink. He sneezed.

"That's the bubbles up your nose," the dancing man said.

Newboy put his jacket on. He couldn't say why he trusted the dancing man, but he did. To a point.

"I climbed Mount McKinley and hiked the Grand Canyon and sailed single-handed from Newport, Rhode Island, to Bristol, England. It's a big world. See as much of it as you can while it's still there. Dinner's ready."

The dancing man served Newboy a plate of baked chicken and brown rice and broccoli, then sat down to the same. Newboy saw that the dancing man was ancient. His skin seemed translucent.

"Where's Stinko?" the dancing man asked.

Newboy's left eye took off for parts unknown.

"You don't talk without him, do you?" the dancing man asked. "I can relate to that. When I lost my feet, I asked myself what I'd miss most. The answer was dancing. Without dancing I'd have no way to express how I feel. If I couldn't do that, I'd have nothing. Dancing transports me, you see. From here to there. To anywhere. I go where my imagination permits me to go, I become who I can become."

The dancing man ate slowly. Newboy vacuumed his plate.

"I decided that no matter what else happened," the dancing man said, "I'd keep dancing after my feet were removed."

Newboy wanted to know why the dancing man's feet had been removed, but not enough to break his vow of silence. He wasn't going to talk again until he found Stinko.

"It's a long story," the dancing man said, as though he could read Newboy's mind. "A piano fell on me." He held out a leg so Newboy could see the artificial foot at the end of it.

"I have special feet for dancing," the dancing man said. "They're lighter. More flexible. They have more spring. If you've lost Stinko, I could teach you a few steps. People always put money in the hat for a good dancer."

Newboy nodded. He wanted to learn. Even though he was sure he was too clumsy.

The dancing man took off the feet he was wearing and put on his dancing feet.

"Everybody can dance," he said. He whirled his way to the dance floor and threw his arms open wide. "You can dance. All you have to do is move with grace and charm, and not fall down."

The dancing man danced a bit of a dance by way of demonstration. He moved like he had wings. He beckoned to Newboy.

Newboy stepped carefully to the gleaming wood floor. He saw his reflection in a wall of mirrors. He didn't recognize himself. The sound of piano and drums and guitars and horns poured out of speakers and filled Newboy's head. Suddenly he couldn't stay still.

"Cast off your lines and let yourself go," the dancing man said. He danced like there wasn't a bone in his body.

Newboy tripped over his feet.

"Close your eyes," the dancing man said. "You'll see

better. Picture yourself dancing and dance to the picture you see."

Newboy jumped about, all bones and sharp angles.

"On your toes," the dancing man commanded. "Dance on your toes."

Newboy lifted himself. The weight of his body shifted to its center. He felt balanced. Lighter. More solid somehow.

"Lift yourself," the dancing man said. "Dance on air. Dance through time."

Newboy closed his eyes and imagined himself moving effortlessly. He jigged and leaped and snaked about like a Slinky toy gone wild. He moved quickly and poetically. Inside himself he roared with newfound happiness.

19 / On the Hunt

Newboy saw light seeping in around the edges of the
board covering the window. It was morning. He'd come
back down to sleep when the dancing man turned off the
music and said the lesson was over. He'd danced for what
seemed like forever by then. He'd been drenched in
sweat and his legs had ached, and his head still hurt from
where he'd been hit, and he didn't care. He could dance.

The dancing man had given him a crisp new ten-
dollar bill. "This is for the performance you and Stinko
put on," he'd said. "You were good. I don't expect we'll
ever see each other again."

Newboy stretched. He folded the ten and stuck it in
his left sock. He climbed out the window into a frigid
rain. He shook himself like a wet dog. He found Silverquick an hour later. In a coffee shop on Broadway. Silverquick was sitting at the counter eating waffles bathed
in chocolate syrup. Newboy went inside and sat next to
him.

Silverquick glanced in his direction, looked away, then snapped his head around. "Couldn't make it on your own, could you?" he asked, syrup dribbling down his chin. "Must be my magnetic personality." He stuffed another chunk of waffle into his mouth. "Have a piece of pie. The banana cream is good. Where's your pal?" He jabbed Newboy in the chest.

Newboy pointed an accusing finger at Silverquick.

"Me?" Silverquick exclaimed. "You think I got Stinko?" He sounded astonished.

Newboy grabbed Silverquick's ear and twisted.

Silverquick punched Newboy in the side, a short chop that forced Newboy to let go. He went back to eating like nothing had happened. "We'll talk when I'm done," he said.

Newboy watched Silverquick polish off the waffles, then lick the plate clean of chocolate. He followed Silverquick outside. He'd worry about getting away when Stinko was safely zipped into his jacket.

"With or without Stinko," Silverquick said, "I can use you. You're not afraid. You got a brain."

Newboy marched at Silverquick's side. They cut into an alley. Silverquick slammed Newboy up against a building.

"I don't like being messed with," Silverquick said.

Newboy struggled. Silverquick's grip tightened. Newboy slowed his breathing, the way the dancing man had showed him. He relaxed his muscles, beginning with his neck and shoulders, working his way down.

"I don't blame you for running from that witch," Silverquick said. "She's a mean lady."

As he relaxed, Newboy felt the pressure on his throat ease off.

"But you're not running away from me," Silverquick said. "You're taking Peeper's place. He was the best lookout I ever had. He decided he didn't want to do it anymore. That wasn't his decision to make."

Newboy raised himself slowly to his toes. Silverquick didn't notice.

"It's too bad about Stinko," Silverquick said. "He was a moneymaker. I heard Smirk's got him. I wouldn't bother Smirk about something like that. I wouldn't bother Smirk about anything."

Newboy closed his eyes. He imagined himself dancing down the alley. He leaped suddenly to his left. Silverquick cut him off. He leaped to his right and started running. Silverquick dove for his legs, but Newboy was too fast. He didn't need those first few steps to get going anymore. Not when he started on his toes. He was off like a streak of light.

20 / Smirk's Place

Newboy entered Old Town. He listened as much as he looked. He heard Hacker coughing. He found Smirk's kids where he'd first encountered them. Hacker sounded like he was going to come apart at the seams he was coughing so hard. The others were giving him plenty of room. Smirk wasn't there. Newboy pushed two garbage cans together to make a windbreak. He found part of a newspaper to put between himself and the ground.

The afternoon passed slowly. From time to time a few of the kids took off. Occasionally they changed positions to talk or conduct business. Newboy dozed. He came awake kicking his feet wildly. An old man wearing many layers of clothing was trying to pry his sneakers loose.

"I thought you were dead," the old man grumbled, annoyed that Newboy wasn't. The old man shuffled off.

Newboy checked his sock. The ten was still there. He snuck a look around the corner and saw that Smirk had arrived. He stood and stamped his feet to get his blood circulating. When Smirk left, he followed. He stayed far enough back so that if Smirk saw him, he could turn away without being recognized.

Smirk led him to abandoned railroad tracks that had become nearly invisible with permanent overgrowth. The tracks brought them to the crumbled remains of a circular brick building that looked like an artifact from an earlier civilization.

Newboy crawled the last hundred yards and peered inside. When his eyes adjusted to the gloom, he saw Smirk. He saw odds and ends of discarded furniture and small piles of personal possessions. He saw Stinko tied to a chair. Smirk was either stupid or crazy. Either way it was trouble.

The kids showed up a few hours later. They ate, then went to bed, wrapped in all they owned. When he was as certain as he could be, Newboy made his way into the roundhouse. He didn't see any lookouts. The chair Stinko was tied to was surrounded by kids. Smirk was stretched out next to it, a sleeping giant who Newboy definitely did not want to disturb. He raised himself to his toes and took a deep breath. He passed inches from sleeping face to sleeping face as he danced his way to Stinko.

Hacker let loose with a string of rapid-fire coughs that sounded like a burst from a machine gun. Newboy went rigid. He went flat-footed. He lost his balance. He started to fall in one direction, pulled himself back, whirled about, then started to fall in another. He reached for things that weren't there. He pulled his body backward against its momentum, trying to alter course. He put his arms out at his sides and held them there like a tightrope walker's pole, until he at last came to rest.

He steadied himself. His body stopped rocking. His heart stopped banging. He listened. Hacker's coughing hadn't disturbed anyone. He reached Stinko and untied the rope that bound him.

"Why'd he tie you up?" Newboy asked inside his head. "What'd he think, you were going to run?"

Newboy looked down at Smirk, whose breathing was as steady as a mechanical pump's. "You probably think Stinko talks by himself too," he said inside his head. He untied the last knot, freed Stinko, put him inside his jacket, and zipped him in. He turned on his toes to re-trace his steps. A huge rough hand closed shut around his leg.

"Got you!" Smirk yelled.

21 / Hacker

"Where's Penny?" Smirk asked, his face stuck right in Newboy's.

"Your breath smells like fertilizer," Newboy said inside his head. He stared directly back at Smirk with his one steady eye.

"Where's Penny?"

Newboy sat in the chair Stinko had occupied, encircled by Smirk's kids. Stinko was still inside his jacket.

"Where's Penny?"

Newboy managed to free his arm from its sleeve. His finger found the loop.

"Where's Penny?" Smirk yelled.

"Penny who?" Stinko responded.

Smirk lit up. "Penny who went with you," he said. "You took her."

"Penny who?" Stinko asked again.

Smirk reached to grab Stinko.

Newboy raised his free arm to protect him.

Smirk batted it away. Newboy winced with pain.

"I didn't take her anywhere," Stinko said.

"Him then," Smirk said, taking hold of Newboy's nose.

"He doesn't know anything," Stinko said with a distinctly nasal twang.

"What happened to her?" Smirk shouted.

"Let go of his nose," Stinko twanged.

Smirk let go of Newboy's nose and grabbed Stinko's head.

"Get your hands off me!" Stinko yelled.

"What are you going to do about it?" Smirk asked.

"If you rip my head off I won't be able to talk to you," Stinko said.

"He'll talk to me," Smirk said, looking at Newboy.

"He doesn't talk," Stinko said. "Let us go. We never did anything to you."

Smirk grabbed Newboy's nose again. He pulled.

"Ow!" Stinko twanged.

"I'm going to make you tell me where she is," Smirk said. He pulled harder.

"You keep doing that," Stinko twanged, "and I won't say another word."

Smirk let go. He hit Newboy on top of the head with the flat of his hand. Newboy heard bells.

"You going to watch me pull the arms and legs off your doll-pal?" Smirk asked. "He'll be nothing when I'm done with him. There won't be enough left to throw away."

"I don't talk without him," Stinko said, "he doesn't talk without me."

"He'll talk without you when I get done," Smirk said.

"Why don't you rip his arms and legs off right now?" Stinko said. "See if I tell you anything then, moron."

"Don't call him a moron," Newboy screamed inside his head. "Stop making him mad."

"He's already mad," Stinko said.

"You calling me a moron?" Smirk asked.

"You have to say things the way they are," Stinko said. "Otherwise, what's the point of talking?"

"Maybe I'll rip the arms and legs off both of you," Smirk said. "Then maybe I'll rip your heads off after that."

Hacker coughed. "Why don't you let them think about it all night?" he said. "Maybe in the morning he'll tell you. If he doesn't, you can rip him apart then."

"In the morning," another kid said.

"So we can see better," another kid said.

"He'll probably wet his pants by morning, he'll be so scared," Hacker said. He coughed. "We'll tie him to the chair."

"Tie them both to the chair," Smirk said.

Hacker wound the rope tightly around Newboy and Stinko.

"Think about what I'm going to do if you don't tell me where she is," Smirk said to Newboy and Stinko.

Hacker knotted the rope five times.

Smirk tested it.

"They're not going anywhere," Hacker said.

"I don't like you," Smirk said to Stinko.

Stinko stared back with his one open eye. He couldn't speak because Newboy's arm was crushed to his chest.

"I like you even less," Smirk said to Newboy. He hit him on top of the head again. The bells returned.

"We're going to fight in the morning if you don't tell me where she is," Smirk said. "Until only one of us is left. Guess which one that's going to be?"

A half hour later they were all sleeping again. Smirk's outstretched hand, its fingers still bent like they were holding on to something, lay open next to Newboy's feet. Hacker coughed, a long, hoarse affair that Newboy thought would raise the dead. Smirk twitched, then rolled over, taking his open hand with him. Hacker coughed again. A kid sneezed. Then it was quiet.

Newboy pushed against the rope with his chest. He twisted his shoulders. He tried to move his feet. Nothing gave. "I'll have to fight him," he said inside his head. "He'll kill me." He heard a rustle of movement behind him. He couldn't see who it was. He felt himself being untied.

Hacker loosened the last knot, then signaled Newboy to follow.

Newboy stood slowly, being careful not to upset the chair or wake Smirk.

Hacker stifled a cough.

Smirk rolled back to his original position. He reached

for Newboy's ankle. Newboy moved the chair. Smirk's hand closed around a leg. Hacker started for the opening at the other end of the roundhouse. Newboy rose to his toes. Hacker coughed a cannon shot. Newboy was sure their number was up.

Smirk grunted, then went quiet. Everybody slept on. And Newboy and Stinko and Hacker just walked right out, nobody the wiser. Their escape was a piece of cake.

22 / Snatched

"This way," Hacker whispered when they were clear of the roundhouse. He ran at an easy gait. Newboy followed. They veered away from the railroad tracks and crossed the seventh green of a long-abandoned public golf course, ran down a fairway, through some trees, and across a narrow bridge. In front of him, Newboy saw a high metal fence.

Hacker was on the other side of it so fast Newboy thought he must have walked through. Newboy climbed it awkwardly, cleared the top, caught his foot on the way down, and landed on his head.

"I'm all right," he said, getting quickly to his feet. He started running, faster now, wanting to put distance between them and Smirk.

They raced through a neighborhood of two-story town houses. They tore up a hill, dashed across a five-way intersection, and found themselves finally on a street lined with auto-body shops and junkyards. Newboy stopped to inspect Stinko.

"He's okay," Hacker said. "I made sure they didn't do anything to him."

"You saved us," Stinko said.

"I don't know your name," Hacker said to Newboy.

"Newboy," Stinko said.

"Is Penny all right?" Hacker asked. He coughed.

"She was the last time I saw her," Stinko said.

"I'm glad you didn't tell Smirk where she is," Hacker said.

"Smirk belongs in a zoo," Stinko said.

Newboy started walking. He took extra-long steps. Hacker had to run to keep up.

"Where are you going?" Hacker asked. There was panic in his voice.

"Getting out of here," Stinko said.

"Wherever you're going, I'm going," Hacker said. "I waited a long time to get away. I couldn't do it by myself. Then Penny went with you. Then you came back."

Newboy wanted to say no. It was supposed to be him and Stinko and Peeper. But he couldn't find Peeper. And Hacker had saved him.

"You can come with us if you want to," Stinko said. "Why not?"

"Why not?" Hacker echoed. He slapped Newboy on the back in fellowship. Then he had a coughing fit.

"We can't stop looking for Peeper," Stinko said.

"If we find Peeper, there will be four of us," Hacker said.

"Four is a good number," Stinko said.

"With four we can look out for each other," Hacker said.

"One more day," Stinko said. "If we don't find him, we go."

It didn't seem right to Newboy to give up. Just because something was risky didn't mean you quit. He'd be careful. He could get through another day. Another one after that if he had to. He rededicated himself to finding Peeper.

"We'll start as soon as it's light," Stinko said.

"Newboy, Stinko, Peeper, and Hacker," Newboy said inside his head. "It sounds right."

"It is right," Stinko said.

Newboy started looking for somewhere to get a few hours' sleep. Hacker coughed a cough that racked his frail body.

"What's wrong with you?" Stinko asked.

"There's nothing wrong with me," Hacker said. "I cough. That's all."

As they walked, sticking to the darker streets so they'd be harder to see, Hacker told Stinko and Newboy his story. There wasn't much to it.

"My father was put in jail and my mother ran away," Hacker said matter-of-factly when he was done. "One morning I woke up and nobody was home but me."

Headlights swept across the street as a van turned onto

it. Newboy ducked behind a hedge. Hacker stayed as close as his back pocket. The van passed. It was an airport shuttle. They walked on. An ambulance brayed its way across the city. Newboy heard glass shatter, then the bawling of a car alarm. In between coughing fits, Hacker filled Newboy's ears with the story of how he knew Peeper, which was from a time before Peeper had been picked up by Silverquick.

Then Stinko told Hacker why he and Newboy were on the run. He told him about the Knoxes and how Mrs. Knox was as bad as Silverquick and Smirk put together. He started to tell him how they'd met Peeper when their story caught up to them.

Newboy hadn't noticed the green van that had been trailing them from a distance, headlights off. He hadn't heard it creeping closer, because he was engaged with Hacker. And he wasn't prepared when it suddenly roared to life and swerved up onto the curb beside them.

The side door of the van slid open, and two men yanked Newboy inside. The door slid shut.

"Hello, darling," Mrs. Knox said, smiling from the driver's seat. "Happy to see me?"

Mr. Knox and the other man had Newboy pressed between them like a pair of pants.

"What's this?" Mrs. Knox asked, plucking Stinko from Newboy's jacket. She held Stinko up in front of her.

"Disgusting," she said. She threw Stinko out the window. She locked the doors, turned on the headlights, put the van in gear, and hit the gas.

23 / Where's Newboy?

As Newboy heard it later, Stinko lay like a pile of rags in the street until Hacker picked him up. If Stinko could have seen out of his one good eye, he would have witnessed the tail end of the van skidding around the corner and disappearing, and Newboy with it. If his chewed-up ears had worked, he would have heard Hacker say to him, "I'll take care of you. We'll find him." If Stinko could have talked, he would have told Newboy the story of how it was that his luck changed.

He would have told Newboy that Hacker put him in his coat and that they started off in no particular direction, with no particular objective in mind, because Hacker was afraid, and he had no idea where Newboy might be, and no idea what to do without him. He talked out loud to Stinko about being too small to take care of himself.

"I can't survive on my own," Stinko would have heard

him say. Hacker had turned ten the month before. He coughed. With his one eye, Stinko would have seen how much it hurt.

They crossed the drawbridge that Newboy had crossed only a few nights earlier when he'd escaped. They made their way to Queen Street. Stinko would have recognized it. He and Newboy had looked for Peeper here before.

"Hey, Hacker!" a voice called out. Stinko would have known right away who it was.

Hacker looked around. He didn't see anybody.

"Hacker!"

He didn't recognize the voice. It could have been somebody disguising who they were. It could have been Smirk. Then again, it might have been Newboy. Maybe he'd gotten away.

"In the alley," the voice called out. If Stinko could have, he would have told Hacker who it was and not to worry.

Hacker wanted to keep going, to find a place to hide until dark. But he also wanted to see who it was. He walked out into the street so that, when he was even with the alley, if he saw somebody he didn't like, he'd have a chance to run.

"Behind the Dumpster!"

Hacker moved closer. He was sure he shouldn't be doing this. He put a hand on Stinko and felt more courageous. He stopped at the alley's entrance.

"Who are you?" he yelled. "What do you want?"

What happened next Stinko would have described as the moment when things started getting better. A head appeared from behind the Dumpster.

"Get over here," Peeper said.

"It's you!" Hacker yelled. He almost giggled. Peeper pulled him from view.

"You see Silverquick anywhere?" Peeper asked.

"No, but he's looking for you and Newboy," Hacker said.

"I'm trying to find Newboy," Peeper said.

"He's trying to find you," Hacker said. He told Peeper about Newboy being snatched up off the street and how he was sure it was the people Newboy had run away from.

"They threw Stinko out the window," he said, unbuttoning his coat. "I can't make him talk." He handed him to Peeper.

Peeper examined Stinko, who lay inanimate in his arms.

"We have to save Newboy," Hacker said.

Peeper stuck his hand in Stinko's back. He found the string and loop.

"I don't know where they took him," Hacker said.

"I do," Stinko said in Peeper's voice.

"Where?" Hacker asked.

"Greenridge," Stinko said. "Two Hundred and Eleventh Street."

"You're almost as good as Newboy," Hacker said.

"I didn't make him talk," Peeper said, handing Stinko back.

"Yes you did," Hacker said.

"I had nothing to do with it," Peeper said.

"Stinko can't talk by himself," Hacker said, buttoning him in.

Peeper started up the alley. "If we're going to save Newboy," he said, "we'd better get started."

That's the story Stinko would have told. It was left to Hacker and Peeper and another time.

24 / Meanwhile

Newboy sat at the kitchen table waiting for Mrs. Knox to deal with him. She was making phone calls and doing paperwork. He waited while she went off on her errands. Mrs. Knox's brother, the other man in the van, kept watch. He looked like his sister, only he was shorter and completely bald. Mr. Knox shook his head sadly each time he passed through. He was sneaky, Mr. Knox. Sometimes he could get halfway into the room before Newboy knew he was there.

While he waited, he wondered. Had Hacker picked Stinko up off the street? He wouldn't leave him there. Not after what they'd been through together. Newboy was sure Hacker would take good care of Stinko. He thought about everything that had happened since he'd run away. It had all been for nothing.

"Why?" Mrs. Knox asked when she returned, like he'd let her down somehow. She carried a bag of groceries in one hand and a sticky bun in the other. "Why can't you be content like the other boys?" She polished off the sticky bun, then licked her fingers. She sat down next to him. She put the hand that had held the sticky bun on top of one of his. He tried to pull away. She was too strong. The sticky stuff from the sticky bun was like paper paste.

He considered for a moment the pleasure it would bring him to say out loud what he thought of her and her husband. He knew they kept a lot of the money the state sent them for the boys. He'd heard them whispering about it late at night. But telling her wouldn't change anything. And she would have heard him speak. His last wall of privacy would be crushed. She'd have access to his thoughts. She'd wear him down. He'd have nothing left of himself. So he kept his mouth shut.

"No more running," Mrs. Knox said. "I won't have my boys running. I won't have the state coming around asking a lot of foolish questions."

She pinched his cheek with her sticky fingers. "They have all these stupid rules," she said. "They don't know their fronts from their backs when it comes to taking care of you snotnoses." She stood and rubbed her sticky fingers on his hair.

"And you're not going to complain to anybody," she said. "Not that it would do you any good. You've been nothing but trouble since you were born. Nobody will listen to you. If you could talk. Which you can't." She smiled and rubbed his hair again.

"Just in case you don't understand what I'm saying,"

she went on, warming to it, "I've had new locks put on the doors and security screens put on the windows. My brother has moved in to keep an eye on you. He's out of work and has nothing better to do. He's going to be your roommate. In the room next to mine."

Newboy spent the rest of the morning stripping beds, washing sheets and towels, then making beds. In the afternoon he washed floors. When the other boys returned from school, he was hit on the bottom with Mr. Knox's belt, once for each day he'd been gone. At dinner he was served an empty plate and made to watch the other boys eat. At bedtime, he was brought to his new room.

"I saved the best for last," Mrs. Knox said. A sliding-bolt lock had been screwed to the outside of the door and its frame.

The room was long and narrow. Its single window was covered with wire mesh. Newboy's cot was against one wall. Mrs. Knox's brother rolled his folding bed in front of the door and set it up. Mrs. Knox closed the door and locked it from her side.

"Sleep tight," she said. "If there's an emergency, pound on the wall."

25 / The Way Out

"How are we going to get in?" Hacker asked.

"I'm thinking," Peeper said.

"How are we going to get him out?" Hacker asked.

"I'm thinking," Peeper said.

"We don't even know where he is in there," Hacker said.

"I'm thinking," Peeper said. "I'm thinking."

"Well, you're not thinking hard enough," Hacker said.

They were hiding in the bushes across the street from the Knoxes' house. They'd found it finally by finding the green van. At last the house was dark.

"Ask Stinko," Hacker said.

"That's crazy," Peeper said.

"Maybe it is," Hacker said, "and maybe it isn't. Ask him."

"I don't know why I'm doing this," Peeper said, taking Stinko.

"So we can get Newboy out of there," Hacker said. He watched Peeper put his hand inside Stinko's back.

Peeper's finger found the loop. "Why don't we try looking in the windows?" Stinko said.

"See. I told you he'd know," Hacker said.

"That was me talking," Peeper said.

"Yeah, but you didn't know the answer until you had him say it."

Peeper thrust Stinko back at Hacker. A car passed. When it was gone they hurried across to the Knoxes'. Peeper made himself as tall as he could.

"I can't get high enough to see in," he said.

"I'll get on your shoulders," Hacker said. He climbed up Peeper's back like he was mounting a horse.

Peeper lurched forward, then backward. "Stop moving up there," he hissed.

Hacker clutched at Peeper's hair, trying to keep from falling off.

Peeper swallowed a cry of pain.

Hacker suppressed a cough.

Peeper stumbled, reached for the house, bent himself in that direction, and finally got his hands on it. He regained control of his body, then realized he couldn't breathe. Hacker's legs were squeezing his neck.

"Letgoofmyneck," Peeper rasped.

"What?"

"Myneck." Peeper pounded on one of Hacker's legs.

Hacker got the message and eased the pressure.

"Now let go of my hair," Peeper said.

Hacker let go. Reluctantly.

Peeper moved to a window. Hacker looked in. "Nobody," he said. They moved to the next window.

"Nothing," Hacker said.

They checked each window in front, then came to the fence. From Peeper's shoulders, Hacker was over it in a second. Peeper was nearly as agile. The windows were closer to the ground here. Peeper, Hacker, and Stinko looked together. Hacker couldn't see much of anything. Peeper saw two people sleeping. Newboy wasn't in the room.

Hacker coughed. It sounded like a bomb going off. He coughed again. Peeper saw movement inside the room. A woman was sitting up. He pushed Hacker to the ground and clamped a hand over his mouth.

"Who's that?" they heard Mrs. Knox call out. Then they heard coughing coming from another part of the house.

It was Newboy. He'd been awake when Hacker coughed. He'd coughed as loud as he could to cover it. He went on coughing, keeping an eye on Mrs. Knox's brother, who wasn't in the least disturbed by the racket. Mrs. Knox's brother had jammed plugs into his ears before retiring.

"I don't like to wake up when I'm sleeping," he'd said to Newboy before turning out the light.

Peeper raised his head and saw that Mrs. Knox was looking at the wall to the next room. "Shut up in there," she yelled in a voice that gave Peeper and Hacker the creeps. Newboy coughed once more for good measure. Peeper watched Mrs. Knox put her head on the pillow.

They moved to the next window. They saw Newboy. Hacker grinned and pointed at Stinko. Newboy grinned back. Peeper signaled Newboy to open the window. Newboy shook his head that he couldn't, then turned in the direction of Mrs. Knox's brother.

Peeper saw right away what they were up against. He pointed to himself, then Hacker and Stinko, then into the house. Newboy nodded that he understood. They made their way to the backyard. The second story offered no possibility of success. They'd need a ladder, which they didn't have. Even if they did, the windows would certainly be locked. Breaking glass that close to Mrs. Knox's bedroom was out of the question.

"Ask him," Hacker said, holding Stinko out in front of him.

"Ask him yourself," Peeper said.

"Okay, I will," Hacker said. He put his hand into Stinko's back the way he'd seen Peeper do it. He fished around and found the string. He pulled on it.

"Try the roof," Stinko said in Hacker's voice.

"Good idea," Hacker said.

Peeper looked at Stinko, then Hacker, then the roof. "How do we get up there?" he asked.

"The tree," Stinko said.

"Good idea," Hacker said.

"You're nuts," Peeper said.

"We climb out on a limb and jump," Stinko said.

"What do we do when we get there?" Peeper asked.

"How should I know?" Stinko replied. Hacker buttoned Stinko in and started up the twisted old black walnut. None of the limbs reached the roof, but one came close.

"No more coughing," Peeper said, starting up after him.

Hacker tested the limb. It would hold them. One at a time. "Wait until I get there," he said.

"Be careful," Peeper said.

Hacker took a step out on the limb. He held the branch above him for balance and slowly made his way sideways toward the roof. The limb began to wobble. His legs nearly came out from underneath him as the limb went one way and the branch the other. He thought he was going to be pulled apart in the middle. He held on and waited until the tree was still.

As he got closer, the limb began to bend. Not much, because he was small, but enough to present a potential problem. He tried to estimate how much farther he could go before it bent too much for him to reach his objective. A few steps later he realized that the branch he was holding on to was coming to an end. He looked over at the roof, surprised to see how steep it was. He might make it, just to slide right off.

He started bouncing up and down on the limb. He sprang off it like he'd been hurled from a catapult. He hit the roof with a muffled thump and immediately began sliding down toward its edge. He spread his arms and legs and pressed his body against the shingles to slow himself. He came to a stop just as he was about to go over. He climbed toward the peak and safety as quickly as he could. He came to a small gable with a window, sat in the space in front of it, and watched Peeper start toward him.

Newboy heard the thump Hacker made when he landed. He turned his hearing to Mrs. Knox's room. She was snoring. Mrs. Knox's brother hadn't moved.

Peeper bounced up and down on the limb, then blasted off and hit the roof. He started sliding. Hacker slid after him and caught his hand.

Newboy heard the second thump.

Hacker showed Peeper the window. Peeper wrapped his jacket around his arm and hit the glass with his elbow. It made a cracking sound. A dog started barking. Peeper removed part of the pane, then reached in and undid the lock. He led the way through the labyrinth of junk that filled the attic. He and Hacker removed the lid from the trapdoor.

"I'll take a look," Peeper whispered. He stuck his head down through the hole and, hanging like a bat, surveyed what he could of the second floor. He lowered himself, then dropped noiselessly.

Hacker landed like a feather. He could feel dust from the attic gathering in his throat. He felt the itch beginning to grow.

Peeper saw that the stairs required great care. He went first. Hacker followed in his footsteps.

Newboy heard them coming. He put on his jacket. He

listened to Mrs. Knox's wheezes and snorts. Mrs. Knox's brother slept on, his mouth opened wide enough to catch bugs.

"I hope nothing flies in there while I'm trying to get out," Newboy said inside his head. He heard the bolt sliding loose. The door opened. Peeper's and Hacker's heads appeared. The door wouldn't open any farther because Mrs. Knox's brother and his bed were in the way.

Hacker coughed.

Newboy coughed louder.

"Shut up!" Mrs. Knox yelled. "I hear it again, I'm coming in."

Mrs. Knox's brother made a series of gurgling noises, then shifted himself so that his face was pointed at Newboy.

"Maybe he's just pretending to be asleep," Newboy said inside his head. "Maybe he's just waiting to catch me." He looked at his friends, then the door, then the bed. There was only one thing he could do.

"If the wheels don't squeak," he said inside his head, "I might be able to get away with it."

He held his breath and took hold of the metal frame. He pulled the bed toward him. It moved. No squeak. He pulled. It moved. No squeak. A little at a time he moved it away from the door. Mrs. Knox's brother turned over suddenly, then came to rest. Newboy moved the bed until he calculated he could get by. He slipped past Mrs. Knox's brother into the hall and locked the door behind him.

Hacker stuck his fist in his mouth to stop himself from coughing. He made small choking sounds. The itch went away and he smiled. He handed Stinko to Newboy, who zipped him into his jacket. Hacker and Peeper started up the stairs, then realized that Newboy wasn't with them. They saw him standing outside the Knoxes' bedroom. They saw him go in.

Newboy raised himself to his toes and made his way to the dresser. Mrs. Knox mumbled something. He reached the clock with the chimes that went off every fifteen minutes. The clock hadn't worked in a long time. He opened the battery compartment on the back.

"Leave me alone," Mrs. Knox yelled without waking.

"Be quiet," Mr. Knox said, still asleep.

Newboy removed the money Mrs. Knox kept hidden in the battery compartment. The dancing man's ten she'd taken from his sock was on top. He put it in his pocket, then counted out the amount he figured the state paid the Knoxes for one month of his care. They'd kept a lot more of it for themselves than they'd spent on him. He put the rest back.

Getting to the tree limb from the roof seemed impossible. It seemed too far away and far too small a target to hit from where they sat on the roof sizing up the situation. And even if they were lucky enough to get there, the limb seemed much too flimsy to handle the force of their landing. On the other hand, what choice did they have?

Hacker ran down the roof to gain as much speed as he could. He launched himself. He landed on the limb, grabbed the branch above him, and made his way quickly to the ground.

The limb bent under Peeper's weight. A disturbing noise emanated from somewhere in its interior. He scrambled off and joined Hacker.

Newboy's finger found the loop in Stinko's back. "How you doing?" he asked.

"I'll be better when we're out of here," Stinko said.

Newboy studied the distance that separated them from the limb and freedom. He looked down at Hacker and Peeper, who looked up at him, expectantly. He fought the panic that was trying to take control. It was a long fall if he missed.

"Think we can make it?" he asked.

"Only one way to find out," Stinko said.

Newboy stood and zipped Stinko in tight. He raised himself up on his toes and imagined his flight to the tree. He soared off the roof, his arms stretched out in front of him, and caught hold of the limb. He hung there, swinging back and forth. One of his hands slipped. He clutched with the fingers of the other. He gathered every bit of strength he had and reached up.

26 / Pink Flamingos

Ten blocks from the Knoxes' house they stopped running.

"We did it," Peeper said, filling his lungs as fast as he could.

"We did it," Hacker said. He was bent over at the waist, hands on his sides, sucking in air.

Newboy unzipped his jacket. "We have to keep moving," Stinko said. "She'll be after us." Newboy and Stinko headed for the highway. Peeper and Hacker fell in at their side.

"Where are we going?" Hacker asked.

"North," Newboy said. Out loud. So they could hear him.

"Hey!" Hacker said. "You talked." He pulled at Peeper's arm. "Newboy's talking." He turned to Newboy. "How come you can talk all of a sudden?"

"Because I want to," Newboy said.

"He talks to me all the time," Stinko said. "Why shouldn't he talk to you?"

"Thanks for busting me out of there," Newboy said.

"It was nothing," Peeper said.

"It was nothing," Hacker said. "We couldn't have done it without Stinko. Why are we going north?"

"That's where Penny lives," Newboy said. "We have to see if she's all right."

"We sent her home to take care of her sister," Stinko said.

"Maybe she needs help," Hacker said.

"That's why we're going," Peeper said.

"We'll stay until we make sure she's all right," Newboy said.

"Where are we going after that?" Hacker asked.

"To the land of pink flamingos," Stinko said. "To sunshine and beaches and no snow."

"And then what?" Hacker asked.

"Is that all you do, ask questions?" Peeper asked.

"A lot of the time," Hacker said. "Then what?"

"Then we'll make some money," Newboy said.

"I'll get a job," Peeper said. "I already worked as a dishwasher once."

"I'll be a street performer," Stinko said.

"I can do something too," Hacker said.

"You'll go to school," Newboy said.

"I like school," Hacker said. "Then what?"

"Then we'll grow up and have a life," Newboy said.

"Sounds good to me," Peeper said.

"Sounds good to me," Hacker said.

"Sounds good to me," Stinko said.

Newboy imagined them living in Miami Beach, in a building they'd find. There would be families. A grandmother would run a school and Hacker would go. Newboy and Peeper would bring in the money. Newboy would work on making Stinko funnier and keeping his mouth from moving. Why not? Who said they couldn't do better?

"Sounds good to me," he said, sealing the bond between them.

He looked back and saw the tops of the city's tallest buildings, their lights sparkling like stars in the blue-black dawn. He hoped his mother was all right. He wished for it. He saw a truck coming. Everything is a chance, he thought. He stuck out his thumb.